## About the author

Anne Nelson was born in northern Idaho and grew up on the lake near her home. She had quite the imagination from the start but never had the dedication to put anything down in writing that was longer than a short story. Still, it has been a dream to have a book published and that dream was made a reality when *All in a Daydream* came out in March of 2020… thanks to Pegasus Publishers.

Now *Dreams Come True*? is going to be her second book in print, her life goal of calling herself an author has come true. So, for Anne, her lifelong dream is now reality.

Recently widowed and starting over has inspired her to keep writing in the hope that more novels will make their way into the hands of other romantics who seek escape, even for a few hours in the pages of a fun read.

DREAMS COME TRUE?

# Anne Nelson

DREAMS COME TRUE?

Vanguard Press

VANGUARD PAPERBACK

© Copyright 2021
**Anne Nelson**

The right of Anne Nelson to be identified as author of
this work has been asserted by her in accordance with the
Copyright, Designs and Patents Act 1988.

**All Rights Reserved**

No reproduction, copy or transmission of this publication
may be made without written permission.
No paragraph of this publication may be reproduced,
copied or transmitted save with the written permission of the
publisher, or in accordance with the provisions
of the Copyright Act 1956 (as amended).

Any person who commits any unauthorized act in relation to
this publication may be liable to criminal
prosecution and civil claims for damages.

A CIP catalogue record for this title is
available from the British Library.

ISBN 978 1 80016 240 2

*Vanguard Press is an imprint of*
*Pegasus Elliot MacKenzie Publishers Ltd.*
www.pegasuspublishers.com

First Published in 2021

**Vanguard Press**
**Sheraton House Castle Park**
**Cambridge England**

Printed & Bound in Great Britain

# Dedication

This is dedicated to all my friends and family who have supported me throughout this endeavour.

# Acknowledgements

Thanks to EL James for the inspiration

# PREFACE

Becca woke with a start and felt very stiff. With a yawn and a stretch, she realized that both her back and neck were way out of sorts.

Plus, she had a weird fucking daydream.

Note to self, 'Never fall asleep in an Adirondack chair.'

She looked up and watched an osprey flying low searching for a bit of breakfast. 'Sushi,' she thought and laughed out loud.

She truly loved this lake and was looking forward to a swim later when the day warmed up a bit. It would definitely help with her sore back and neck.

"Damn chair."

No longer able to stay in the chilly water for hours like she had as a child, still, after fifty plus years, the lake still brought her the peace she cherished.

Just a little over a week and a half more and she'd be heading back to her realty.

You know... work, bills and the day-to-day world of responsibilities.

Well, that thought sucked!

*Don't misunderstand, she loved Alaska and her life in Sitka, which was part of the Inside Passage, and a rainforest, which some people didn't know.*

*She also loved being able to teach the next generation of sales and marketing executives, but she also treasured her summer break back in the lower forty-eight.*

Spending time on her lake.

It really gave her the best of both worlds.

Usually when she was on her summer hiatus, she'd spend a couple weeks in Nevada with her best friend.

But cancer took her eight months earlier.

Just that memory brought tears to her eyes.

*Mary was Becca's very best friend for over twenty years. Her sounding board, her confidante, her sister from a different mister and the one who convinced her to get a divorce sixteen months prior and to find the happiness she deserved. Find love.*

She was still working on the last part, a promise she made to Mary just a few days before she died.

Damn she missed her friend, so very much. It always made her heart hurt and it was one of her deepest fissures... she wondered if she'd ever feel whole again.

She also figured that she'd never be able to fulfill her promise. Too old and far too much of a cynic to believe that there was one love out in the world just waiting for her.

Shit like that was for daydreamers.

She was a realist.

The tears came. 'Damn it'. They often did when she thought of her bestie.

Her sip of coffee was less than pleasant as well: it was cold.

"That's disgusting!"

And then she questioned to herself:

'Wow, I wonder how long I was asleep?'

She rose to go refresh her cup and grab a tissue when she heard that annoying sound.

Jet-ski… the quiet breakers on the lake.

She wasn't a fan.

Not her concern right now, coffee was her only agenda. Well, that and a Kleenex.

Suddenly the irritating sound ended and that did catch her by surprise. Jet-skis don't just stop unless a rider has been thrown off or they stop suddenly.

She turned to see if everything was all right since it sounded close.

Damn close apparently, since there at the end of her dock was a very handsome man smiling at her.

The sun was making his green eyes sparkle and then in a very pleasant baritone voice he spoke. "Would a lovely lady spare a cup of coffee, bit cool on the water this morning?"

'Nice smile' she thought. And nodded.

*While growing up on the lake her mom and dad always had an open-door policy when folks came by the cabin. She remembered many a beer getting thrown to a passing fisherman in the late afternoon. Or welcoming an early riser for a cup of coffee. The world was simpler back then. You didn't have to watch every word or action for fear of offending someone. You never worried for your personal safety either.*

*Simpler times back then. Many would argue better. Less complicated was more Becca's sentiment.*

BUT something about this chance encounter was different and seemed memorable. She felt a connection to him.

Definitely a déjà vu moment.

She shook her head. 'Focus, Becs...' right, coffee. "How do you take it?"

He was walking towards her and pulled her into a very unsuspecting hug. And it felt nice. And oddly enough, it didn't feel awkward.

Actually, it felt scary familiar... 'What the fuck?'

When his strong arms released her, he explained. "Sorry, you just looked like you needed a friendly hug." And wiped away a tear on her cheek.

He really did have quite a nice smile and was way handsome.

She thanked him for being so incredibly thoughtful.

She pointed to her coffee cup.

"I take a little milk in my coffee, thanks. I'm Curtis by the way, Curtis Kane."

She nodded as she headed up to the cabin. "I'm Becca."

# TUESDAY

While getting their coffee ready, she couldn't shake the feeling that she'd met him before. It seemed all too recognizable. But how could she forget that exquisite face.

His was indeed very striking. She'd always been quite partial to bearded men with blue or green eyes and his were wrapped up in a very nice six-foot frame. And that smile of his could melt the tundra.

So, with coffee in hand, Becca headed back to the dock to her waiting guest.

She handed him his cup and he thanked her again and hoped she didn't mind his intrusion.

She just smiled and shook her head. It was always nice to have company. She didn't really know the neighbors to the west of her cabin very well, weekenders for the most part and the ones to the east weren't there but once maybe twice the whole summer.

*Their cabin was actually built by her grandfather years and years ago. She wished it was still in the family, but her grandmother had other ideas and sold it when Becca was still in junior high. She was the real boss of their marriage. And the sale broke her grandfather's heart.*

*He was a very kind man and loved his grandkids unconditionally, she didn't know many like him and while visiting her cabin she would frequently venture up to the high meadow and talk to him.*

*His ashes were there along with some of her mom's and dad's. It was a very peaceful place.*

*They put her grandmother's ashes in the lake.*

*Her grandfather deserved his own peace in the afterlife. She smiled at the thought.*

"You look lost in reflection. May I ask what gave you that lovely smile?"

She was embarrassed for ignoring her guest.

"I am so sorry. I was just thinking of my grandfather. He built that cabin up on the hill for he and my grandmother and helped my dad build the original A-frame for our cabin. He was one of my favorite people that used to roam the earth."

She took a drink of her fresh cup of coffee. So much better when hot.

He smiled at her again and asked why she was crying earlier. If she didn't mind telling him.

She wasn't sure why, but she didn't mind at all. "I was thinking about my best friend. She died less than a year ago and I just miss her." She tried to fight back the tears for the second time in one morning. Nope.

'Fuck.'

He reached over and wiped them off her cheek again and told her he was sorry for her loss. He then reached over and kissed her hand.

'What a sweet gesture,' she thought.

And still she was getting no weird vibe from him. He seemed genuine. 'Huh!'

The oddity of it all make her compelled to change the subject so she asked him where he was staying on the lake. And what brought him to this part of the world. Simple and straight forward enough.

"I have a boat I'm staying on. We just finished building a yacht for a client in the area, so we're taking her out for a shakedown cruise before the owner gets here the day after tomorrow. I was testing how far the jet-ski goes on a single fill up when the cool morning brought me to you." He was beaming. A proud papa for sure.

"You design and build boats for a living?" She was curious and it sounded interesting.

He nodded.

"What do you do when you're not playing hostess to passing strangers?" He lifted his cup to his very sensual lips.

'Focus, Becs, he is so out of your league.' Good reality check.

She told him she taught a marketing class at the local university in Alaska. She also told him that she used to live in Juneau but when her mom got sick, she needed to come south and, after she passed away, she found a job in Sitka a couple years back. Way more information than she usually gave to a complete stranger, but it again didn't feel uncomfortable, and he seemed truly interested.

"Is your dad still around? You mentioned he built your amazing cabin. I really love these older rustic places around the lake."

"No, he died a few months after mom. Just went to sleep and didn't wake up one day. I think maybe he died from a broken heart. Their ashes are up in the meadow with my grandfather's. And this place is full of so many memories, I feel much closer to them when I'm here."

He took her hand into his and gently squeezed it. "Again, I'm so sorry for your loss."

She smiled and nodded.

When he released her hand, she sort of wished he hadn't, it felt nice. He then passed her his empty coffee cup and asked if he might come back the next day for another cup.

She nodded. "If you're in the area... come on by." She hoped that sounded casual. Her heart skipped an extra beat at the thought. 'What in the world is happening to me?'

He smiled that glacier melting smile and gave her a kiss on the cheek before getting back on that ever so noisy contraption and headed back across the lake.

Well, that was definitely a different start to her usual day on the lake.

With his return the next day she'd need to have some questions about boats... after all there were hundreds if not thousands in south-east Alaska. All sizes and kinds. Maybe he'd have to deliver one of his creations to her neck of the woods one day.

That pleasant thought put a huge smile on her face.

'Come on Becs, get your ass in gear. And men that look like him aren't interested in women who look like you.' There's an in-your-face realization. She hated her subconscious some days, the bitch.

With that inner monologue finished, she headed back to the cabin to get into the shower and have some breakfast.

*At this point you should know that our Becca has lost sixty-five pounds over the past seven plus months by not eating bread, pasta or potatoes. But still wanted to drop another twenty, even though she was feeling pretty fit with all the swimming and walking she'd been doing the past several weeks.*

When she had tested her blood sugar levels that morning before coffee, they were a tad low so, after her shower, she fixed herself a bigger breakfast than usual. Todays consisted of two poached eggs on two slices of tomato.

She also took her daily medication.

She had type two diabetes and her numbers had been excellent these past several months… on occasion a tad low as mentioned earlier. Nothing overly serious though.

*Mary was always the one who got on her to take care of herself.*

*Her big brother, James, took up the mantle from time to time but it was different coming from him. He hated her dieting all the time and told her that's why she become diabetic in the first place. Yo-yo dieting, he called it. Gaining and losing all through her life. He was probably right… jackass.*

But in truth they were both right and getting healthy was important. Not at all the reason for her current weight loss. Still.

Thinking about her brother made her realize that he would, in fact, be arriving Friday night, she figured she'd better do the shopping and laundry by Friday morning.

No need to rush to town. Time on her lake was a much more enjoyable thought.

After breakfast she took a few minutes and called her landlady in Sitka.

Clara was an elderly native woman, one of the elders in the Tlingit clan, who rented Becca a nice room at a very affordable rate and in turn Becca would run errands, took her shopping and to the odd medical appointment that her son, Douglas, couldn't take her to.

She also kicked Becca's ass at cribbage on a regular basis.

She adored Clara and worried when she was away for so long.

She'd always try and call at least once a week to check in.

It rang only once before Douglas answered.

"Hi, it's Becca. Is your mom okay? I just wanted to do my weekly check on her and let her know I'll be back the Sunday after next."

He told her his mom had the flu but was fine and he'd let her know of Becca's call. He asked if she needed a ride from the airport.

He could be very sweet and was the same age as her brother James, fifty-nine.

She let him know that she didn't and to take care of his mom and hoped he didn't get sick and with that exchange, they said their goodbyes.

Clara hinted more than once that Douglas needed a good woman in his life. Becca knew he drank like a fish and had no interest but always grinned at the matriarch and told her she wasn't ready for another relationship.

But thanked her anyway.

Of course, all the thoughts earlier of her parents and grandfather made her trek up the hill for a nice long visit.

The cabins around her were usually empty during the weekdays and way too busy during the weekends so she liked to take advantage of the quiet time.

*A lot of her neighbors rented their cabins out to what the locals called 'weekenders', she was never a fan since many partied too loud and broke the rules of the lake. Her brother agreed with her about NEVER renting their cabin to anyone. Family only!*

Becca always wondered if she'd be locked away for talking to the dead.

It's not like they talked back so she thought not but laughed at herself anyway.

After spending some quality time in the meadow, she walked down the road for a mile or two to stretch her legs.

She saw a few deer and lots of squirrels but no signs of bear or cougars. In truth, she'd not seen any predators in several years.

Still, she always carried mace just to be safe.

Once back at the cabin she grabbed her suit and went for a nice long swim. Always one of her favorite parts to the day. And, as predicted, it helped work out all her kinks.

She'd been swimming in this lake since she was eighteen months old. Born under a water sign… she lived up to being a true water baby.

Her folks had one helluva time getting her out of the water all through the summer when she was young, but now her bones were a tad older, and the water was a tad chillier so about forty or so minutes was about all she could take at any given time.

She was also too old to lay on the dock, so she opted to sit in a chair and let the sun warm her up.

She heard a jet-ski in the distance and smiled.

NO, she still hated them for their noise but didn't mind the very cute rider she'd met that morning.

Again… this all seemed so weirdly familiar to her.

After enough sun for one day, Becca headed back inside. She grabbed a cold bottle of water and an apple and settled in on the couch for a bit of light reading.

The rap on the door scared the shit out of her.

No one ever came without her hearing them.

Hell, there was a wall of windows in the living room, how did she not see them?

Shaking her head, she went to the door, also fully glassed, and there was the ever-attractive Mr Kane.

"I hope I didn't disturb you. But we're finished with the yacht and were planning to take my boat on a tour of your lovely lake tomorrow and I wanted to invite you to come with us."

His boat was a thirty-five-foot Bayliner and quite nice to look at since it was right in front of her dock.

"She's a lovely boat but I don't really know you that well…"

He interrupted her.

"A day on the water would change that, don't you think?"

He had that amazing smile plastered on his face. And continued his reasoning with barely a breath. "There are only three of us on the boat, the engineer is my best friend and co-owner of the business, his name is Carl Franklin, and his life partner is our resident cook and bottle washer, Warren Clark." His look was so hopeful, and his smile was back.

She nodded since it sounded a lot safer once he told her who else was on board. Plus, she really did like going out on a boat.

That and she was a very good swimmer. Worse case, she'd jump overboard.

"I promise you'll be perfectly safe. You won't need to find an escape route. Pick you up in the morning, eight o'clock, if that works for you?"

Again, she nodded having another odd déjà vu moment.

He pulled her into a hug and told her to have a pleasant evening and off he went.

Seriously, what just happened?

How did she not hear that boat?

Where in the world did this man come from?

She had a date for tomorrow. Really?

She shook her head in disbelief.

This kind of thing just didn't happen to her.

Yet it just did.

Freaky Fucking Tuesday!

She opted for a SlimFast protein shake for dinner and an evening swim to clear her very confused mind.

She channel surfed for an hour and decided to head for bed since a good night's sleep was in order before her day on the water.

Well, that and she wanted to get up and pack her own food since most people don't know how to feed a diabetic and she was even more unique.

The lapping water on the shore lulled her into a nice sleep.

# WEDNESDAY

When she woke it was light out and the bedside clock read, twenty after five.

Too early, but since she needed to pee and had managed a good night's sleep, she figured that she might as well get her ass up.

The cabin was chilly so, after her bathroom duty, she started the fire.

She loved a roaring fire.

*It brought back wonderful memories of when she was a child.*

*Her dad would have the cabin nice and toasty before anyone even thought of getting up. Back then, he went to town every weekday to work, and her mom would give him a list for that evening's meal… just an A-Frame back in those days and space was very limited. Life was so much simpler back then or at least it seemed that way to her.*

Fire going and pleased she didn't burn herself — she'd done it on several occasions before — time to get some coffee brewing.

Still a bit early and chilly to drink on the dock so she opted for a shower… but first things first, test numbers.

Oh… that's a tad low. 'Shit'.

So, food first and then shower.

She wasn't that hungry, so she went for half of a KIND bar, and she'd wait on meds until later in the morning.

Once showered and dressed in shorts, top (a tank top under a light cotton button up) and sandals, she poured herself a nice hot cup of coffee. Most certainly her favorite part of any morning — caffeine.

She grabbed her sugar free creamer out of the door and noticed that the fridge was indeed empty of food. Just a few eggs, a couple of protein shakes and two apples left.

Since she had lots of time to kill, she might as well make a list for Friday.

The sun was waking up but there was still a chill in the air, and the cabin was nice and warm, so she decided to forego the dock completely and sit at the kitchen table.

She knew what her brother liked to eat so that went to the top of the list and then she added items that she was willing to consume. Those two never went hand in hand.

*By all rights James should weigh over three hundred pounds the way he ate but no, he carried maybe an extra fifteen or twenty pounds and had his whole life.*

*If she even looked at a Snickers bar, she seemed to gain a pound. So not fair.*

The knock on the door made her actually jump… followed by a very audible, "FUCK ME!"

Yep, her very early guest was none other than the very attractive Curtis Kane.

She was thinking of making him wear a fucking cowbell. Damn!

With her heartrate slowing down a bit she went and opened the door.

"Good morning Becca. I'm so sorry I startled you. But if that last part was an invitation… I'm totally game." Huge grin and a wink.

Her look was less humorous. "Yeah, no. But feel free to help yourself to coffee and you are way early."

He just shrugged at the last comment and went and fixed himself a cup. He also shook his head when he looked into the very empty fridge.

She noticed. 'Hey, at least there was half and half for your coffee. So, suck it up buttercup.' She usually tried to make her snarky remarks in thought only. That one made her smile.

He asked if she'd like to sit in the living room and she nodded in agreement since her grocery list was mostly complete.

He padded the seat on the couch next to him and again she couldn't shake the feeling that this had happened before.

"Your refrigerator is virtually empty… what do you eat or were you planning on going to town today? I noticed your shopping list. I know we invited you on the trip around the lake, but I don't want you to go without supplies." He looked concerned.

How very odd.

Not really his business.

She shook her head and told him she was fine and was planning a trip to town on Friday morning before her brother arrived for the weekend. And then informed him not to worry, the freezer had food as did the pantry, which in fact they did but nothing she'd eat, little white lie.

'Nosy fucker.'

She hated being asked about food or her lack of it.

*Her size was currently a twelve to fourteen, but she was looking to be more like a ten to twelve. Doable, she'd been there before... just never could maintain it. She tended to be an emotional eater.*

*That all changed when her world collapsed around her ears eight months earlier. Mary's death put her in a tailspin. She still hadn't found her way back.*

*Now food was her enemy, and it took everything she had to consume anything. She used the guise of low carb and getting healthy to get people to 'shut the fuck up'. And butt the hell out of her life.*

She came out of her thoughts with him staring at her and she apologized. Again, not used to having guests she tended to veer into her own little world.

Putting her hostess hat on she decided to open up a new conversation.

"So, Curtis where is this new boat you designed and built anchored since I don't think you own Bayliner. And on that note, what's the name of your company, where is it located and why don't you use one of your own creations?" She loved that smile.

"It's just outside Hope and our company is 'C&C Design', based out of Bellingham, Washington." He took a drink of coffee before continuing.

"It's a small company and we've built forty boats over the last nineteen years and designed over a hundred others, which doesn't sound like a lot, but it really is. And my boats are too expensive." He winked after the last statement.

He again looked like a proud father and that amazing smile never got old.

"Sounds like a lot of boats to me. And you seem to love what you do which makes it even better. I'm also sure Bayliner is relieved they can compete." She smirked at him.

He nodded and laughed at her comment.

The sun was finally wide awake, the sky was blue, and the winds were calm. Looked to be a great day for their venture on the water.

"Can I get you a refill?" Her inner hostess was fully awake, about time.

He shook his head. "You go ahead, and could you please tell me your full name, have you ever been married, your age and are you seeing anyone?"

Huh?

Seemed like normal questions in the scheme of things.

She went and got herself another cup of coffee first. One cup seemed insane to her. She would take it intravenously if possible.

"It's Rebecca Lynne Jackson, Jackson being my married name. I divorced just about a year and a half ago. I was thinking about going back to Sims but it's just a name. And I don't answer to Rebecca so if you wish to stay in my good graces, it's Becca. I will also tolerate Becs. Age is just a number baby, but I am older than you. And for the last question… other than you… no one." She was quite pleased with her last statement since it could be interpreted in many different ways and with that, she took another sip of her fresh cup.

He smiled and told her he hadn't been with anyone in over thirteen months now and would like to get to know her better. And promised to always call her Becca since being in her good graces was very important to him. He also told her he was forty-four and would have guessed her age to be two or three years older at most.

'Oh, is that what he meant by seeing anyone.' Well, that didn't come close to what she meant on any level. To answer correctly, with his train of thought, is totally different and something she wasn't prepared to tell someone she'd met the day before.

Physical relationships weren't on her agenda and hadn't been for going on fifteen years now.

She liked that she looked seven years younger than her fifty-three years. But wondered all the same if she should tell him to go away.

'And what did he mean by knowing her better?'

"Becca, you keep leaving our conversation. I get the impression you over think a bit too much." His look was more than quizzical.

She nodded since in truth she really did.

She decided to change the subject completely once again.

"I need to pack some food before we go. How long do you think we'll be on the water?"

"My best guess would be six or seven hours at the most, but we have food, and you don't, so we'll be happy to feed you. Unless you need specific food. Are you vegan?" His look was more curious with a touch of wariness thrown in for good measure.

She told him she was diabetic, and it was just easier to bring what she was willing to eat and went and grabbed the small cooler off the back porch. Four waters, a protein shake, apple, the rest of her KIND bar and an ice pack to keep the contents cool and she was ready for the day.

"Seriously that's all you'll eat for the entire day? I don't think so Becca. That's not even close to enough calories." He actually looked miffed.

Odd reaction since again it was none of his business.

She could only hold her tongue for so long so, with a touch of sass, she told him, "It's enough for me or I can stay here, and you and your overstepping attitude can go jump in the lake."

She was so done trying to impress him, or anyone for that matter.

'I'm too fucking old for this shit.'

His shocked look made her laugh, and he grabbed her cooler and her hand and headed out the door.

She looked back at the almost extinguished fire and managed to pick up her keys and turn off the coffee pot before she was escorted out of the cabin.

He waited for her to lock the door and headed to the dock, the Bayliner was there to pick them both up. She assumed it was Carl at the helm.

Curtis hadn't spoken since they left the cabin so maybe it was his turn to over analyze the situation. She was thinking she could always jump.

He introduced her to Carl and Warren, and they made an adorable couple. Warren was very flamboyant, and Becca liked him right off.

Carl was a bit harder to read but still very cordial.

Curtis handed Warren the small cooler.

Carl asked her if she broke Curt since he also noticed his friend and business partner wasn't really speaking to anyone.

She shrugged since she may have.

His laugh brought Curtis around since he slugged Carl in the shoulder before heading up to the fly bridge to take over the steering duties.

Warren handed her a life jacket which she took but her look was utter bewilderment.

So were her thoughts. 'Weird. Why would anyone need a life jacket on the lake?'

Carl asked her to please put it on for safety reasons. She was regretting her decision to come with them since they were all a bit overbearing.

Still, she put on the superfluous item without fastening and continued standing in the back of the boat looking around.

At this point she was really considering jumping and swimming back to her cabin. 'Fuck her cooler'.

About that same time, Curtis came back down and took her hand bringing her up to the fly bridge next to him and proceeded to fasten the life jacket for her.

His look was stern but somewhat sexy she thought.

Still, she shook her head at the whole bizarre situation.

The Bayliner had a good speed for such a big boat and if they didn't go around the whole lake, they should be able to make the loop in just a few hours.

'Crap.' She remembered that her phone was still on the charger at the cabin. That was disappointing. No pictures.

Or any way of calling and arranging an escape route. Plus, she didn't take her meds, so she'd have to be extra careful about eating anything. Not that hard actually. Her appetite died with Mary.

She very much wanted to smack the cute man at the helm since it was his early arrival and departure that made her forget her phone and pills. She again was regretting coming.

After twenty minutes, the silence was a tad deafening, so she got up to go find her cooler and to get a bottle of water, well that and get away from the very moody but stunningly cute captain.

He reached out and took her arm asking her to not move around when the boat was at its current speed.

'Oh, for the love of God.' She knew how to hang on when a boat was moving, she'd been on enough of them in Alaska, but sat back down to appease him.

*Yes, she rolled her eyes. Wouldn't you?*

The minute he slowed for another boat's wake she bolted down the stairs and took off the stupid life vest as she entered the main floor living area.

'Nice.'

Cute little galley, dining area, small living room with a TV that was way too big for the space. 'Boys and their toys.' More importantly, her cooler was there.

She went and got a water and sat across from the dining area.

Warren was in the galley getting breakfast ready.

He asked if she was hungry, and she said 'no' but thanked him all the same.

Carl came up from where the sleeping accommodations were, he told her there were two heads when and if she needed them.

She nodded.

*Those are bathrooms for non-boat folk.*

"So, my guess is, you pissed Curt off." She liked Carl better now. He didn't beat around the bush.

"Apparently," she smirked.

Warren laughed and asked if they could please keep her.

That made all three of them laugh.

She knew he couldn't hear them with the noise from the engines, but he must have sensed he was the topic of conversation since the boat slowed to an utter stop.

She waited for the wake to catch up to them and it did. Lifting the boat up and down for roughly five seconds.

Yep, been on many a boat before.

Warren took that opportunity to fix breakfast plates for the three men and suggested he and Carl eat up on the fly bridge when Curtis came in looking… well, curt.

He took his plate and sat at the dining table across from where Becca was sitting.

She broke the awkward silence. "Are we going by Garfield Bay Marina by chance?" She knew they weren't that far.

He just nodded.

'Good' she thought. She could disembark there and get a ride back to the cabin.

She was way too old for this crap.

"You aren't hungry? I wished you'd eat something. It's going to be a long day. And please don't leave the upper deck again when we are in motion, it's dangerous." He took a quick breath.

"And I don't want you to get off the boat at Garfield Bay either." He smiled. But it wasn't the one she liked.

She just shook her head.

He was very perceptive.

"I guess that will depend on your silent treatment. And an FYI, I'm nine years older than you. Been on a boat before and swam in this lake since I was an eighteen-month-old." She did like Curtis, but he was... quirky.

That should be PC enough.

He in turn informed her that she would wear a life jacket if on deck, he would continue to insist she eat more, and he would try to keep his temper in check and not be so brooding.

'Good compromise... except for the life jacket and eating part but it was only for a few hours.'

And she never said she wouldn't get off the boat if given a chance.

"Do you prefer Curtis or Curt? I noticed Carl refers to you both ways and I was wondering if you have a preference?"

She liked looking at him. His bald head fit his frame and those green eyes were stunning. Plus, he had dark eyebrows and beard that gave him an almost fierce look and like she thought before, very sexy indeed.

"Truth is I prefer Kane." He noticed her appraising him. Oops!

Her heart skipped… damn. Total déjà vu moment, for the third time.

She nodded and was slightly embarrassed for being caught staring.

She liked the idea of calling him 'Kane'. But why?

Wow, she seriously needed to figure this out before she went bat shit crazy.

Freaky Fucking Wednesday.

He finished his meal and went and put his plate in the sink. He then took her hand to lead her down to the sleeping quarters.

"Thought I would show you the whole boat." His grin was a tad disturbing.

'Not that big of a boat… hundreds just like it all over Alaska.' But she let him give her the tour all the same.

She really did live too much in her head.

Becca was surprised by the size of the full bath. Roomier than the one at the cabin even. The berths were on the smaller side and there were only two. The second head was much smaller but worked for its main purpose.

The biggest surprise was how incredibly clean and tidy the boat was for having three men on board, she figured Warren was to thank for that.

Nope, according to Kane, Carl was the total clean freak. Go figure.

In the bow was a hatch leading to the front deck of the boat. He cornered her there and gave her a very nice kiss. His hands traveled down her sides and onto her lower back where he pulled her very tightly against his chest as the kiss deepened. This caused her to gasp, and his tongue took full advantage of the opening. Becca's body's response to his was shocking to her since it had been a very long time, but her head wasn't going to let anything else happen.

She was too old to be that easy a fuck. Been there, done that and it took her almost four years to get over the self-loathing.

Of course, she was only twenty at the time. But still.

She ended their kiss and went to leave.

He didn't try to stop her but asked her what was going on in that head of hers?

He pegged her for over thinking again.

YEP!

Very perceptive.

"Becca it was just a kiss. It didn't have to be anything more. I didn't bring you onboard for sex. Just to get to know you better." The look he gave her was hopeful.

To her that seemed strange in so many ways.

"My body's reaction to yours was disconcerting to me. And I'm just not ready for anything close to that kind of intimacy. It's been a very long time. So, when it comes to anything physical, I let my brain now rule the show. And you're right, it was a very nice kiss, thank you. And you were doubly right, we are so not having sex." And with that she headed back to the main salon of the boat.

Once she retook her seat, he leaned over and whispered into ear, "I liked it too and I would like to kiss you a lot more. I'll be happy to wait until you're ready. But I thought you said it was just over a year, like me."

She shook her head.

"You're not going to tell me, are you?"

And again, she shook her head.

He made an exasperated sigh.

He took her hand once again and led her back up to the fly bridge so the boys could go back below.

*And yes, she had to wear the stupid life jacket.*

Once ready, he put the boat back on step and headed around Picard Point to the largest and widest section of the lake and continued down the neck, which is actually the deepest.

Her lake was in fact quite massive.

He also bypassed Garfield Bay and smirked about it. 'Jackass'.

They ran for another hour and a half to Cape Horn where Kane headed across the lake to the opposite side and continued their trek around.

It was beautiful on the water and Becca really wished she had a camera.

She'd been around the lake several times throughout her life but each and every time she seemed to discover something new. Today was no different.

Their ride had been nice and smooth thus far since there wasn't much boat traffic on Wednesdays.

After another hour Kane slowed and asked if she'd like to take a dip to cool off at Granite Point? He wanted to give his boat, as well as himself, a bit of a rest.

She nodded but mentioned not having a suit.

He'd rushed her out of her cabin earlier so she didn't have a chance to grab one, but she knew she could swim in her shorts and tank top… figuring she'd have more than enough time to get dry.

He, of course, told her that she could always swim in just her bra and panties.

'HELL NO,' was yelled in her head.

All he saw was a coy smile and a shake.

She liked her legs and ass, but her midriff was not meant to be seen. Could be an issue if and when she ever did decide to have sex.

Right, who was she kidding?

*Yet… that kiss?*

Her lake was fed by the surrounding mountains and their many rivers so it was usually chilly but in the deepest section of the lake, she imagined it would be even colder.

She was right.

Not being bashful she removed her cover shirt, keys to the cabin and sandals and dove off the back swim-step without a care in the world.

'Fucking cold,' was her first thought but she swam away from the boat ten or so yards and began to acclimatize to the temperature.

Damn she loved her lake.

Kane yelled at her to come back to the boat.

*I'm sure you could imagine that this was quite confusing since he just said they were going swimming.*

*He was nothing if not a conundrum.*

Becca easily swam back and looked up at his pensive face.

"You just said we were going swimming. What's up?" She was getting frustrated with all his miscues.

"You don't have on a life jacket. Please get out of the water and put one on before you go back in." That stern look was back. Somehow, at that moment, it had lost its sex appeal.

Without over thinking she said, "You have got to be fucking kidding me. Who swims in a life jacket? Wouldn't that just be floating?"

With that 'in your face' tête-à-tête, she took off again but this time underwater. She popped up about twelve or so feet away, smiled and waved at him.

He was looking almost angry, and she couldn't have cared less.

Her lake wouldn't hurt her. And he needed to seriously lighten the fuck up.

Thank God Warren came out and jumped in, with a life jacket on. She was right… it was more floating than swimming. He just sort of bobbed up and down. She couldn't help but be amused. But, at least with him in the water Kane calmed down, a little.

Of course, he handed Warren another floatation aid to bring to Becca. She took it shaking her head. 'Damn he's anal.' An upgrade from quirky. And not in a good way.

Once Kane was out of sight she swam back to his boat and climbed up onto the swim step.

*Hell no, she didn't put on the idiotic thing.*

When he returned, she was just dangling her feet and lower legs in the water and enjoying the sun beating down on her.

That insipid life vest was sitting beside her.

He still looked miffed and again she smiled at him.

He shook his head and jumped in the lake… his gasp made her laugh. Didn't he realize how cold it would be.

He didn't stay in long.

*And yes, he was wearing a life jacket. 'FREAK!'*

Carl appeared and handed her a towel; she thanked him and made her way around the boat to lay out on the bow to dry off completely. And perhaps avoid Kane in the process.

Win-win!

Or he might join her. How lovely.

Nope, not so much!

'I need off this fucking boat.' She glared at him.

"I have one rule Becca 'life jackets', and you can't seem to follow that simple request. You seem to have a knack for pissing me off. Why?" He actually looked both stern and baffled.

She looked right at him and told him that his rule was stupid. Boat in motion she'd wear the damn thing. Boat not in motion when everyone was going swimming, no floatation aid needed or required.

Again, a bit 'in your face' reply.

"I so want to take you over my knee right now. You're infuriating." And with that he got up and left her alone on the bow.

'How Christian Grey of you,' she thought and actually laughed out loud. She'd read the *Fifty Shades* trilogy not that long ago. It was one of Mary's favorites.

'I am seriously way too old for this shit.' She shook her head.

It was a few moments later when she heard another boat coming closer. This actually surprised her since they'd seen less than a half dozen the whole day thus far.

When she glanced back, she realized it was the sheriff's boat.

That put a huge grin on her face, and she made her way back around to the stern.

She waved to the younger man on the approaching craft.

It was her nephew, Jake and his partner in crime, Justin.

*They had been best friends since middle school, went through the police academy together and then ended up as partners in the sheriff's office. Both were single and loving it. Justin was actually three years older, but you could never tell. He didn't have the best start in life and ended up getting held back, twice. If anyone ever said anything, Jake would beat them to a pulp.*

*Jake also has an older brother, Mark, who was married with three kids and when Becca's brother asked Jake when he was going to finally settle down, his response of, 'Never I hope', always made her a very proud aunt. She loved his free-spirited attitude. They had always had a close relationship. She really loved the little shit.*

"Hey, Aunt Becs. Just checking to make sure you all didn't break down or something." He looked at her suspiciously and very surprised.

"Hi, JJ… nope all good, just stopped to take a quick dip." She'd always referred to them as one unit. Even as kids.

Justin couldn't help but chime in. "Becca, how do you know these gentlemen? I don't believe I've seen this boat on the lake before."

She loved that they were trying to be protective.

*No, not at all!*

"I don't... they kidnapped me off my dock this morning." Her teasing smile told them she was fine. And to watch their step.

Jake shook his head at his playful aunt. "Really Becs... three guys and one girl? It's a fair question."

"Do you think I need more? How Bohemian of you." She gave them both a 'don't fuck with me' look.

"Go away JJ. Find some poacher to arrest and I'll see you both Sunday for the barbeque."

With that they waved and headed back towards town, a good three-hour run at their top speed.

She turned to see all three men staring at her. Warren was trying not to laugh, and Kane had a weird smile.

Shit, she didn't introduce. 'Fail on common courtesy.'

"Sorry... that was my nephew, Jake, and his partner, Justin. Should have done introductions... my bad." She gave them all a wicked grin since she really didn't give a damn.

And with that, turned and headed back to the bow.

Carl brought her a life jacket as Kane started the engines and they were back underway.

At least she got to stay on the bow for a little while.

She put on the damnable thing to appease the domineering skipper.

They were going much slower... she had a feeling it was because of her.

'Let's not prolong this fucking voyage any longer than necessary!'

She reached over and was pleased to find the hatch was unlocked and climbed down inside the boat... discarding the life vest in the front hold.

Once she used their facilities she went up and grabbed another water and her apple from the cooler.

Warren was back in the galley. 'Poor guy, is that all he gets to do?'

He told her that he was fixing tacos with beans and rice for lunch, and she thanked him again but was perfectly fine with her apple.

She put the towel down first since her shorts weren't quite dry and sat at the dining table looking out at the lovely view.

Kane came down from the fly bridge in a huge hurry and was shocked to see her sitting there.

His sigh told her that he didn't see her go through the hatch. 'Oops'.

"Could I please get you to eat more than an apple?" He looked stern but hopeful.

'How cute.'

"What did you have in mind Mr Kane?" she raised both eyebrows and licked her apple.

That actually caught him off guard and he blushed.

He smiled her favorite smile and shook his head before heading back up top.

That got Warren laughing.

Mostly talking to herself, "Wow, he seriously needs to lighten the fuck up."

Yep, Warren had full on giggles.

She went up top when lunch was served.

It did look and smell good but that amount of carbs could only be consumed by, well them apparently. She tended to get sick if she ate too much. Another reason to watch her food intake.

Kane left her alone about eating at the urging of both his shipmates. Smart man.

Becca almost wished she had gone with her nephew but since he was on duty it wasn't allowed.

'Maybe I should have spat on him, and he could arrest me.' That silly thought made her smile.

This day just keeps getting longer and longer.

She was bored and Curtis wasn't really talking, again.

'Moody fucker.'

After lunch the boat was back up to full speed and looked to be heading to Hope.

Great, now she'd get to see his creation.

PLUS, her cabin was only a forty-five-minute run from there.

Even better.

His sudden voice startled her out of her train of thought.

"Would you mind coming over and steering for a while?" He was almost smiling.

'Wow, trusting me with his boat.' That actually shocked her.

She nodded and took the captain's chair.

He pointed to where they were headed and left her alone up on the bridge.

She was very okay with that too.

'Maybe it's his time of the month.' Again, she laughed out loud. Not like anyone could hear her over the engines.

She'd been at the helm for quite some time; in fact, they were now less than ten minutes out of Hope when he finally returned.

He apologized for leaving her for so long but something in their lunch hadn't agreed with him.

He also told her not to use the smaller head for a bit.

She laughed... very courteous.

After handing her another water and the rest of her KIND bar, Becca gave him back his chair with a 'thank you'. Kane pulled her into his arms giving her a very nice kiss. He was a very good kisser.

He slowed the boat down and pulled her into a more intimate kiss and this time she had no issue kissing him back.

Truth be told, she liked him so much better when they were nonverbal.

He was back to wearing her favorite smile when they looked at each other.

"How long has it been Becca?"

She rolled her eyes and shook her head as she took the co-captain's seat.

She shoved the remaining KIND bar in her pocket for later.

He gave another audible sigh and got the boat back up on step.

When they rounded Warren Island, she couldn't believe the size of the monster yacht. It had to be over one hundred feet in length.

Kane slowed down so he could dock at the back of the beast.

"It's fucking huge… why in the hell is she on this lake? A boat that size should be in the ocean. You built that behemoth? Damn." She felt like her eyes were about to pop out of her head.

His expression was flattered and amused.

"Well, I didn't expect quite that reaction but she's here because the new owner lives here. And I firmly believe he's showing her off. But I totally agree that she should be in the ocean and it's my understanding they are moving her in the fall and heading to the Hawaiian Islands sometime in late November." When he glanced over, Becca was still staring at the huge vessel.

"She's one hundred and ten feet and the biggest we've ever designed and built. Took us the better part of two years." He was beaming.

She was still shaking her head when he continued.

"Do you want to see the inside? And Becca would you please stop saying fuck." He was back looking stern.

"PRUDE!" She liked shocking him.

She took the steps down to the back deck where Carl and Warren were standing and removed that stupid life jacket.

"Beautiful isn't she." Another proud creator.

She nodded.

Kane backed his boat to the swim step of the yacht like he'd done it a thousand times. The yacht's name was 'Daddy's Girl'.

Cute with a slight 'ick' factor.

Kane's boat was named 'Precious' a bit too *Lord of the Rings* for Becca's taste but what the hell, none of her concern.

Her tour began in the engine room… Carl's baby and he was very pleased. It was massive and took up the bottom level just below the waterline. He was going on about the computer program he created that could run this huge beast with just a few people. She got lost in his techno jargon but nodded and smiled just the same.

The next level was where they entered and housed a smaller boat, four jet-skis, two kayaks and a bunch of other items in storage containers.

One flight up from there was the crew quarters. Four berths, a small galley, seating area with couch, TV and two chairs and a back deck with a few more chairs and a small table.

One more level up was the main salon, and it was massive. Full-sized galley, dining room, living room and three staterooms. The master suite had a full-sized bathroom plus two walk-in closets.

The next floor up had a very nice back deck with seating for eight to ten, BBQ, hot tub and, further toward the bow, was an entertainment room, another bathroom and small gym. The bow offered lounge chairs for sunbathing.

The top level was all bridge with a back deck that had enough room to land a helicopter.

Colossal and impressive!

Becca told both Kane and Carl that she was a beautiful boat, and that the new owner should be thrilled and if not, he was a fool. They both beamed with pride.

She now felt as though she was on private property and just wanted to head to the cabin.

They'd been on the water for just over six and a half hours now and he must have sensed she was done.

He reached for her hand and led her back down the four flights of stairs and onto his boat.

"I'll take you home, but can I ask a favor as well?" Such a hopeful look.

She nodded.

"May I come and spend the day with you tomorrow at your cabin?"

"Kane, if today was any indication, we really don't get along all that well, why would you want to spend more time with me?" She was more than a bit curious.

He reached over and gave her another very nice kiss. "You are an enigma and I still want to know you better." He winked at her.

She rolled her eyes for the fifth or sixth time that day.

"Fine but we're not having sex so you might want to get laid before you come over." And with that declaration, went to get her last bottle of water from the cooler.

As he walked by her, he patted her ass. "How do you know I was even going to offer?"

She shrugged since that was actually true but, if his kisses were any indication of his intent... then sex was on his agenda.

He took the seat next to hers as Carl started up the Bayliner and drove away from the massive leviathan.

He held her hand the entire way back to the cabin.

"Becca, tell me how long. It can't be that bad."

She sighed. 'One-track mind.' "Okay, out of curiosity... what would you consider long or bad?"

"Well, right now, I'm thinking thirteen months is damn long, but I guess three years. Anything over four or five could be bad. Everyone is different though. And since I don't know your situation, you're the only one who can judge what 'bad' is to you."

Nicely stated Mr Kane.

She really didn't want to have this conversation.

He was like a dog with a bone… wouldn't let it go.

'FUCK IT.'

He raised his eyebrow like he knew she had said the 'f' word in her head.

Again, FREAK!

"Fine! But if I tell you, you have to sit there with no reaction, or this will be the last time we will see each other. I am totally serious. You will not be welcome at my cabin again, ever. Do you agree to those terms?"

He nodded but was no longer smiling.

She shook her head not believing she was going to actually tell him. She also didn't believe that he would be able to keep his mouth shut. And she wasn't kidding about her conditions.

'This is beyond the stupidest thing I've done in a while.' Still, she continued. "The last time I had sexual intercourse was just over fifteen years ago."

She waited. Truly and utterly amazed that he kept his word and just sat there with no reaction whatsoever.

'Good boy,' she thought.

*Well of course she couldn't resist teasing him. Fish and a barrel come to mind.*

"It's killing you, isn't it?"

He nodded.

'Serves you right, Mr Fucking Nosy.' Again, snarky in thought only.

She saw her cabin coming up. The trip was almost over. 'Thank God.'

Pulling her hand free she said, "Listen, you seem to be a very nice man, Curt, and I really hope you find someone to share your life with. Some leggy blonde perhaps that will fuck your brains out. Thank you for the day on the lake and the tour of your creation." She kissed him goodbye and grabbed her cooler.

Once on the back deck she easily stepped off the boat onto the dock before they even came to a stop.

She pushed the boat off and waved goodbye to Carl and Warren.

Kane was now there with a very odd expression.

'Lighten the 'fuck up' dude... and this is why I will never be in another relationship. Sorry Mary.' She sighed.

She shook her head to regain her senses, turned and headed up to her cabin. She needed something for her headache and probably should check her blood sugar levels again.

Becca could tell her numbers had fallen so she ate the other half of the KIND bar Kane had handed her earlier but only after taking some Tylenol.

She tested a bit lower than that morning. "Well, that sucks out loud."

She decided to omit any meds that day and an hour later she drank the protein shake that was still in her cooler.

Feeling much better, she took a late afternoon dip without anyone bothering her and called it an early night, deciding to read in bed.

Sleep came before the end of the chapter.

# THURSDAY

Becca woke the next morning with a start. The clock read six, so she knew she slept through the night. So, why was her heart beating so hard?

The second knock on her window explained the reason.

Who the hell would bang that loud?

'You've got to be fucking kidding me.' She was going to kill him.

She pulled open the shade and there he was... Mr Curtis Kane. She shut it again and wondered if he'd go away.

NOPE!

She grabbed a flannel shirt and went and opened the door.

"What could you possibly want this fucking early in the morning Kane?" She actually raised her voice.

"Good morning to you too and I've asked you not to use that word, it's beneath you." His displeased look was trumped by her angry one.

"If my language upsets your delicate nature... don't let the door hit you in the ass on your way out." She slammed the bedroom door and locked it.

She was thinking of going back to bed, but now that she was totally pissed off, there would be no sleeping.

She tested her numbers, and they were better but not great.

She made the bed and changed into jeans and a long-sleeved T-shirt.

When she came out, he was busy making a fire.

Becca decided she needed a vat of coffee and made a full pot that morning. Then ducked into the bathroom to pee, brush her hair and wash her face.

Feeling a bit more put together, she still wanted to kill him.

'We are totally not right for each other. He really needed to go find some thirty-five-year-old nymphomaniac and get totally fucked.' That thought made her smile.

As she emerged, he stated, "The boys dropped me off and are heading to City Marina to get the boat ready to pull out on Sunday so I'm all yours for the day."

Damn that smile.

She wasn't buying it.

"Thanks for getting the fire going. You want coffee?" It came out a bit snippier than she intended.

But then again, he had arrived rather early with no warning and woke her up, not that she'd have slept much past. Still!

She figured he had to have planned his appearance and their departure. 'What game are you playing now, Mr Kane?' She wished she'd never told him.

"Is there any way you won't be pissed at me all day?" The dumbass look he gave her made her laugh.

She poured two cups of coffee and handed him the half and half while she doctored hers.

She headed into the living room and sat in the chair across from the couch.

*Oh yeah... still pissed.*

"What's up with you and life jackets anyway?" She had wondered all day yesterday but never asked.

He went on to tell her about his childhood friend who drowned in front of him on Lake Washington. He can't get past it and needed everyone he cared about to wear one when on the water. It was not as bad near shore, but he still stressed and watching her swim yesterday almost killed him, mentally.

"I am sorry for your loss. Therapy might help. Really good drugs might as well. And since I had no clue, it was not my intention to stress you out." Explained a lot but she still wondered what he wanted.

He patted the seat next to him without responding to her remarks.

She shook her head.

'Hell no.' He wasn't getting forgiven that easily.

"Don't you have a big ass yacht to show to the new owner today? What are you doing here, Kane?" Her tone was a tad less harsh. Coffee helped with that.

He was smiling her favorite smile again. "He took ownership at five a.m., he's quite the early riser. Wrote us a check for the final installment, which Carl has, and

I couldn't leave without seeing you again. Becca, I quite like you if you hadn't noticed. And yesterday, you told me to find a leggy blonde and I have." His eyes sparkled. And again, he patted the seat next to him.

She had a little blush going but nodded and smiled back.

She did think he was very handsome, and she enjoyed his kisses but there were a quite a few miles between Sitka and Bellingham... not to mention British Columbia.

Plus, he was nine years younger... which made her an actual 'cougar'.

She took another sip of coffee and made the decision to forgive his early arrival and went and sat on the couch.

Still over thinking.

He lit up like a Christmas tree. She laughed but accepted his good morning kiss. It was very nice.

She intentionally threw off his game plan. "I'll be happy to drive you into town so you can meet up with Carl and Warren whenever you want. Not a bad idea to get groceries for my brother's arrival tomorrow night and I need to fill some water jugs anyway."

He again didn't respond to her remarks. Instead, he took her face in his hands and gave her another kiss, followed by another and when her body started to respond, his tongue took full command of hers and she didn't stop him this time.

It felt really good, and her head now wanted it as much as her body.

'Traitor.'

"Becca, I really want to take you into the bedroom. Would you be okay with that?" His eyes looked like they adored her.

That can't be right!

"So, that's why you came here? Thinking I'd be a quick and easy fuck! I don't need your pity. I'm not interested in being a notch on anyone's belt or some charity case." She pulled away feeling flush from her anger not embarrassment.

His shocked and hurt look made her take a different tone.

"Kane, like I stated yesterday, you seem to be a very kind and sweet man; plus, you're successful and beyond good looking. Go find someone younger than you, not older. Someone that lives, I don't know, within two hundred miles would be a good start. And yes, I'm well aware that my body responded to yours in ways it hasn't in years. But in saying that, I just can't handle any more pain in my life." She was fighting her emotions and distracted herself with another sip of coffee.

She was beyond frightened at the thought of intimacy. And as stated, couldn't or wouldn't be anyone's one-night stand.

He took her cup and put in on the coffee table and then pulled her into a huge hug, cradling her in his arms.

She felt very safe there.

And it again, felt familiar.

Yep.

Freaking Fucking Thursday.

"First off, woman, I didn't come here for a quick fuck. That would be an insult to you as well as me. Secondly, I don't know who the hell hurt you this bad to make you think you don't deserve to be loved in every way possible. I would never intentionally cause you pain. And thirdly, Becca, I want you and as you just stated, you want me too so maybe we can see where the day takes us and could you maybe not over think what may or may not happen. I'll be fine to wait for you to tell me when you're ready for the bedroom." He kissed her forehead and stroked her hair.

"I thought you didn't like the word, fuck." And she smiled into his chest.

"I don't like you saying it. In fact, I'm thinking that every time you say it today, I'm going to smack you on your backside, hard." He was also smiling.

She then leaned back to look at him. "If you hit me, I will mace your ass. But as long as sex is off the table until I'm ready, you can stay."

His expression made her laugh.

Still, he nodded in agreement.

"Sweetheart, I would never hit you. But a well-placed smack on the ass can be stimulating, trust me. Or just an attention getter. You'll know the difference. And if all you want to do, is sit here on the couch and talk all day, I'm good with that. We could even make out a bit, whatever you're comfortable with."

She relaxed in his arms.

"Becca, I don't want you to stress about anything." And with that gave her a very sensual kiss.

She didn't object. It felt nice. And she happily returned that affectionate gesture. As stated before, she liked him nonverbal… a lot.

When he started to kiss her neck, asking if that was okay, she nodded. He moved up to her earlobes his tongue darted into her ear and sent shivers throughout her whole body and again he inquired if she was fine with what he was doing. She told him yes, it felt nice.

She was no longer feeling the tension about being too close to him. She was becoming utterly aroused by this man's expert lips and tongue.

DAMN!

His hands moved to her breasts, and she could feel his erection against her leg. She was quite flattered that she was turning him on too.

That also hadn't happened in years and years.

Maybe she did have a bit of sex appeal left.

Becca had forgotten how amazing it could be to have someone hold, caress and love her.

It felt good and, for once, she didn't over think. She let the feelings blossom.

"Can I take your shirt off please?" She nodded. And with that he pulled it off to gain access to her breasts with his hands, lips and tongue.

OH MY!

The sensation was almost overwhelming.

All her earlier concerns about being a quick and easy fuck were gone. He was seducing her, and she was enjoying being incredibly wanted and desired. Again, that hadn't happened for a very long time.

Her moans seemed to fuel his attack on her breasts, giving her a very unexpected orgasm.

'HOLY SHIT!'

That was new and something she'd never experienced before.

He gave her a smile and another passionate kiss.

She smiled back and feeling rather inspired, she made a very bold request.

"I would like another one of those please."

Kane stood, held out his hand and pulled her into a very nice embrace. With her permission, he escorted her towards the bedroom.

"It will be my pleasure sweetheart. But I am curious, how many orgasms have you had with all your sexual partners?"

Her answer of 'three' made him seem almost irate.

His lips retook command of hers as he shut the bedroom door.

'FUCK ME!'

She woke up nestled in his arms with her head on his chest. She'd never experienced anything like that before. He was relentless and, as promised, gave her several more orgasms.

She was feeling very sated and a tad sore.

But happy beyond belief.

She seriously didn't think things like that were even possible.

Books of course or dreams, which were both utter fantasies.

'Shit…! That's it!'

She had dreamt of him.

He was her erotic daydream just two days prior.

The details were all fuzzy but that explains her constant déjà vu.

Mystery solved!

She wasn't going nuts…well that's up for debate.

But the revelation let her relax and settle back into his arms.

While he slept, she was remembering each and every kiss he'd given her, his tongue all over her body and his fingers, oh my… and that stirred her again and she was wide awake with desire.

What had he done to her?

She'd never felt so turned on.

Was there an off button?

Did she want one?

His hand caressed her back, letting her know he was awake, and it moved down to her bare ass, and she moaned and kissed his nipple.

"Is my beautiful girl ready for more?" She was.

He moved on top and slid deep inside her.

Becca liked how they fit, and he didn't leave any room to spare.

She wrapped her legs around his lower back and they both enjoyed giving each other a very powerful climax. She had several aftershocks by the time he finished.

"Damn woman, I wish I could keep this up for the rest of the day, but I am a mere mortal and in need of food and water." He pulled her into his arms.

"But if you're agreeable we can resume in a few hours." He was smiling her favorite smile.

"Death by orgasm is sure to make an interesting obit." She was teasing him, and he winked.

He got up, buck ass naked, and she saw his full physique. 'Fuck he's gorgeous.' And she was surprised that appendage of his actually fit inside her.

WOOF!

"Admiring the view sweetheart?" he grinned at her as he slipped on his jeans.

She just nodded quite enthusiastically with her own revealing smile.

He then went into the dresser and found a red baby doll nightie that she knew wasn't hers and tossed it to her.

"That's all you'll need to wear for the rest of the day." And with another wink he walked out of the bedroom.

She blushed but tried on the very revealing piece of cloth.

It didn't really fit and left nothing to the imagination, barely covered her own bare ass and her front was quite exposed with the low-cut V-neck.

She wondered who it actually belonged to?

Before she could change into something else, he was back and caressed both her breasts and grabbed her ass nodding his approval of her attire.

'Damn that man.'

She took her robe off the back of the door before leaving the room feeling slightly aroused, again.

As she moved, she realized that she was also quite sore.

He didn't say anything about adding the robe to her attire, which she appreciated. And then got busy searching the freezer for some food she could fix for him.

Pleased to find a steak and some frozen potatoes, they made her wonder what the hell to feed him later, if he was still there.

'Come on Becs… no negative thinking right now.'

She snagged her second-to-last protein shake and drank it while getting his meal ready.

It dawned on her that she'd not eaten anything that day. Oops.

Once the steak was in the microwave defrosting, she got the potatoes on the stove for a quick fry and then into the oven to stay warm while she cooked the steak and the last of the eggs. A small stove required that she do everything in shifts.

She even found some English muffins and butter in the freezer. 'Thank you, big brother.'

Kane was in the living room channel surfing and drinking his second bottle of water.

WOW, she wasn't the only one that got a bit wore out.

That made her feel good.

When she looked out the window, she was surprised to see his Bayliner approaching the dock.

Huh?

"Kane, you have visitors."

He came into the kitchen with a more than a confused look and she pointed to the dock.

He shook his head and headed out the door.

She took a moment to enjoy the view of him in just jeans descending the stairs before she turned the pan to low and headed into the bathroom.

'Jeez I look totally fucked,' she laughed at herself.

She didn't say it out loud.

After washing her face, brushing both hair and teeth and using the facilities she emerged to find both Carl and Kane in her cabin.

Damn. Now, she was really glad she put on the robe.

"Tell her why I have to leave." He was looking quite pissed at his friend.

Carl appeared totally embarrassed. "I am so sorry, Becca, but the owner of the new boat called and is having a couple issues that we have to address now, or he threatened to cancel his final payment."

Seemed reasonable to her… it was their reputation on the line, not to mention their livelihood. She nodded.

She reached up and gave Kane a tender kiss and told him to go find out what's going on with his baby. And then asked Carl if he'd make sure Warren fed Kane an extra hearty lunch… he needed to keep his strength up. And winked.

He blushed again, nodded and bolted out the door.

'Such a girl,' she just smiled.

Still, it reminded her of someone. She shook off the wayward thought.

Kane went and got his shirt and shoes and gave Becca a very passionate kiss letting her know he'd be back, and she wasn't to change clothes while he was gone.

With a quick slap to her somewhat exposed ass, he headed down to the dock. And off they went towards Hope.

'Damn he was right. That was more arousing than painful!'

She put his half-cooked steak in the fridge, the potatoes in a bowl to finish up later and grabbed her last apple to munch on.

After a half hour of channel surfing, she was bored and decided a swim would be a great tension reliever and may slow down her sexual appetite that Kane was nice enough to increase by tenfold.

The lake was cool and inviting and she swam down to the small bunkhouse about one hundred and fifty or so feet away from the dock. Sort of her version of laps.

On the second leg she heard her phone. 'CRAP.'

She knew she'd never reach it before whoever was calling hung up, so she finished her swim and climbed up on the dock and grabbed her towel.

She made it up the stairs when it rang again and caught it in time to see it was her brother calling.

She picked it up and answered on speaker and took it outside since she was still dripping from her swim.

"Hey James. Did you just call a few minutes ago?"

He had and wanted to let her know he wasn't going to make it to the cabin the following day liked planned. His delay was due to a meeting with the planning commission that got moved up a week, but he would try and be there by two or three on Saturday afternoon. He didn't have to be back to work until Tuesday so they would still get a nice visit, just a bit shorter. He also asked if she'd please make him their mom's fried chicken for dinner. She, of course, told him she would.

And made a mental note to add that to the grocery list.

His drive from Billings, Montana was just over eight hours, so his timeline seemed about right. And since he owned the company, she wondered why he had to return so soon.

Still, it would be nice to see him, even for only a day or two.

"You could have texted me that. What's up?" She knew her brother.

"I talked to Jake this morning and he said you had a new guy in your life and being the ever-nosy big brother, I wanted to know about him and make sure you're okay. Becca, going out with three strangers on a boat isn't a great idea in this day and age." He liked to play the protector and she wasn't a fan.

*At this point you should know that James has always gone by his given name. He in fact hates nicknames for himself but gave Becca hers.*

*Which was fine since she hated her full name.*

*But little sisters love to push buttons.*

"You listen to me Jimmy... I'm over fifty now and can take care of myself and you can remind that overstepping nephew of mine that paybacks are a bitch. I have pictures of him naked in the bathtub from middle school and I'm not opposed to posting them all over Facebook on his next birthday." She wasn't really mad... more flattered but he couldn't know that.

He started laughing and told her he'd pass her threat along and not to call him Jimmy.

They said their goodbyes and she went back down to the dock to get a bit of sun since she was slightly chilled.

The upper deck didn't get sun until later in the afternoon.

She was almost dry by the time the Bayliner returned. Kane jumped off and the boat continued back towards town. Carl and Warren both waved to her.

He bent down and gave her a very nice hello kiss and told her he missed her.

She was glowing.

"Missed you too. Did Warren feed you? Is your lovely boat, okay?" She took his hand when offered and he led her back up to the cabin.

"Yes, and yes. Now let's get back to our day together." His smile was a tad roguish.

He made short work of her swimsuit and undressed a bit slower so she could enjoy the show.

Even better!

Nope, the swim didn't curb anything... she was alive and eager when his lips and tongue were back on hers.

Damn, his stamina was beyond amazing, and she was feeling very spent and, again, thoroughly fucked.

She also lost count of the orgasms, okay not really, five but still...

He got up and got them both a cold water and returned to cradle her in his arms.

She really liked this man and hoped he'd stay the night.

And wondered what his thoughts on that subject were.

"Are you over thinking again sweetheart?" She shook her head and played with his chest hair.

He patted her ass and told her to stop wondering if he was sticking around. "I have no plans on leaving you anytime soon."

She had to ask how he knew that's what she was thinking.

"Becca, for whatever reason, you think you don't deserve to be loved and you're totally wrong, so it was an educated guess. I very much enjoy having sex with you and I will continue to do so for as long as humanly possible. So, get used to me being around woman." And with that, he slapped her ass with an audible whack and, although it stung, she again felt slightly aroused.

'Not at all like hitting. Maybe saying fuck out loud was a good idea.' She was grinning.

His hand came down again and this time he caressed her after. She again felt her body craving him.

What had he done to her?

The next slap and her moan fueled him, and she couldn't contain her want for him. It was almost primal, and her release was almost violent.

When she woke it was just getting dark outside and she was alone but could hear him in the kitchen.

She smelled the steak he was cooking. It smelled divine and she felt bad for not fixing it for him.

'Bad hostess Becs.'

When she went to move, her body expressed some discomfort. She was sore... really sore.

Her moan wasn't sexual at all, and he called for her to stay put.

She thought an ice pack between her legs might feel good.

He surely had to be the envy of almost every guy in the country.

Again, WOOF!

'Wait... my lake.' She smiled at the idea of the cool water.

Forcing herself up, she took the robe off the back of the door. No weekenders around... she wasn't opposed to skinny dipping.

"Hey beautiful, I almost have dinner ready and you're going to eat." Such a sexy look disguised as stern.

She nodded and headed out the front door.

His hands were a bit occupied so he couldn't stop her.

By the time he got out on the upper deck she was enjoying the cool lake and swimming out her stiffness.

He took the towel off the railing and headed down to the dock.

"You broke my vagina Mr Kane." But her grin gave away her sheer delight in the thought.

"Out. Dinner is ready. And it's not broken, just out of practice." His wink told her they may not be done for the evening.

She swam farther away from shore.

He was laughing at her. "Okay, please don't go out any farther and if you come out now... we'll watch a movie or read a book. As long as you're in my arms we can do whatever you want."

She returned to shore and wrapped the towel around her. Kane picked up her robe as they went up the stairs.

She shared his steak and eggs but wouldn't touch the potatoes or muffin.

She did the dishes since he had cooked, and he built them a nice evening fire.

As promised, they cuddled on the couch and found a movie to watch. They made out a bit too and that was just fine with her.

Her final thought that night. 'Thank you to whatever entity who sent this amazing man to me.' She slept encased in his arms. Safe, warm and completely sated.

# FRIDAY

When her eyes finally opened it was bright outside.

The sun was fully up, and the clock read eight.

She hadn't slept in that late in quite some time.

Anything past six thirty was decadent in her mind.

It was then she realized that Kane was right beside her, still fast asleep. She couldn't help but smile.

He needed his rest.

Before getting up she covered him with the blanket and as quietly as she could made her way to the kitchen.

Dealing with a nature call first, she then started coffee, tested her numbers and went to get a fire going.

It wasn't that cold in the cabin at this hour, but she loved a morning fire.

When his arms came around her, she jumped. His lips were on hers and the thought of an actual fire went on hold since she was having a bit of a firestorm raging internally.

What that man could do to her with just his tongue should be illegal.

Catching his breath he said, "Get your pretty ass back in that bed, now."

She was breathless herself and just nodded as his hand connected with her ass.

'Fuck that's hot.'

His tongue, lips and fingers aroused her moments after they were back in bed.

His moans, like hers, fueled both their sexual appetites.

She felt every pulsating thrust and her body matched his as they both relished their release. She couldn't remember ever being that vocal during sex… Holy shit!

"Damn woman. That was incredible. I am looking forward to the next several hundred of those." He was rubbing her back.

She kissed his chest.

"Well, that is an insane number of orgasms. I hope that you meant over time. Or are you really trying to kill me?" She smiled as she looked up into his eyes.

"No sweetheart, they won't kill you… but I am look forward to giving you each and every one of them. Let's just call it due diligence for your other inept encounters." His tender kiss was so wonderful.

"Kane, you don't owe me anything. And what you've already given me, I'll cherish forever." She settled back into his arms.

"Becca, that almost sounded like a goodbye. I told you, I'm not going anywhere." He moved down to get access to her breasts and began to caress her which was such a turn on.

He stopped just long enough to ask, "What time is your brother coming?" He was spreading open her legs to continue his quest without waiting for her to answer.

DAMN! AGAIN?!

Holy hell where did his stamina come from?

She started to moan, and he was back inside her.

She screamed with another climax, and he followed suit.

"Kane… please… I don't think I take any more. You're an incredible lover but you're seriously wearing me out." Her breathing was back to being a tad erratic.

"I am impressed you've taken as much as you have."

He gave her a very passionate kiss and she responded in kind.

"Becca, your brother's coming, right? If we don't get up soon, he may find us here in what might be considered a little awkward situation." He was trying to gauge her mood since she hadn't moved.

She shook her head. "Coming tomorrow now."

He kissed her forehead. "Bed it is."

They both drifted off to sleep.

She woke with the sun high in the sky and feeling very sore, but her body still wanted him.

How could she possibly be horny after their morning of serious fucking?

They should get up and go to town for groceries.

She was enjoying caressing his chest and playing with his nipples when he woke.

"Kane, if you tell me how to do it right, I'd like to try oral sex on you for a change." She looked at his face for acceptance.

"Sweetheart, did someone tell you that you did it badly?"

She nodded.

He pulled her up to the pillows and even with his face.

She was waiting for him to say something but instead he took her lips to his and they never spoke.

Moans don't count.

He was finally worn out, about fucking time.

No pun intended.

Becca was beyond sore. Happy and content but sore.

Kane informed her they were in fact getting up and heading to town for groceries.

She agreed. More so now since he gave her what her body craved.

Him.

Up, showered and dressed. They both ate one of the last two KIND bars as they trekked up the hill to the SUV. He wasn't a fan of what he called camping food.

With empty water jugs and the laundry loaded, time to head to town.

Becca also remembered to bring the list she made the other morning. She'd forgotten on a few occasions and ended up missing something each and every time.

Not good with town being twenty miles away.

Kane didn't just ask to drive, he told her if he couldn't he'd play with her breasts all the way to town.

'Blackmail... really, jackass.' Yep, snarky in thought only.

He drove.

Topic of conversation on their forty-minute-drive into town.

"Becca, how many men have you slept with?" He glanced over to her.

She didn't miss a beat. "Four including you. You?"

She really did like surprising him.

Still too familiar.

Freaky Fucking Friday.

"Many more than four. How long did they last? I know the third was your husband and I'm assuming he's the asshat that told you how bad you were at oral sex?" He was holding her hand now.

Her first thought was, 'They should have had this conversation before they had sex.' But, if they had she might have changed her mind. She wasn't proud of her first couple sexual encounters.

He squeezed her hand and told her to stop over thinking.

She smiled since he was again right on target.

"The first was in college and it was a very quick one-night stand. Truth is, I wasn't sure we actually did anything. A few years later it was a weekend pickup and then you know the third." She wanted this inquiry to stop.

"Okay, but why a few years between one and two and the last question about this subject is why fifteen years without sex? Industrial accident?" He was trying to make light of the one he knew caused her the most pain.

She laughed at the attempted joke.

"Self-abhorrence mostly. Wasn't proud of getting drunk and letting my guard down, I didn't really even know him. And since it wasn't a satisfying experience, I wasn't in any hurry to do it again. As for the last question, the asshole ex drank a lot at the beginning of our marriage. When he stopped drinking, I didn't want him to touch me again, ever. He couldn't remember all the horrid things he said and did, and I couldn't forget." She shook her head but finished the tale.

"His health took a turn shortly after and he lost his sex drive with all the medications he was taking so it became a nonpoint." She was looking away from him as she retold that story. It was a sad, pathetic and infuriating subject for her.

He pulled over and pulled her into a very loving kiss.

"Why in the hell did you stay with him?"

She floored him again.

"I didn't have you." And returned his kiss with her gratitude for him being a persistent and gracious man.

He intensified their kiss and said that was the nicest thing anyone had ever said to him.

How could he arouse her so quickly?

'Fuck!'

He raised his eyebrow like he knew she thought the 'f' word.

'FREAK!'

Back on the road and heading to town gave her time to settle her desire and get back to their tasks.

"Kane, with your sexual appetite, why thirteen months?" She figured it was only fair for her to ask a personal question or ten.

"Nasty break-up and a huge ass boat to build." He gave her his favorite smile.

She nodded.

Once in the little hamlet, Becca got the laundry going first thing and Kane filled the water jugs.

He also spotted the Arby's across from the laundromat and took off while Becca waited for the towels, sheets and a few pieces of clothing to wash.

When he returned, he had two very large roast beef sandwiches, a grilled chicken salad and two bottles of water.

She didn't even attempt to argue and ate every bit of her salad after thanking him.

Once the laundry was in the dryer, she went over the grocery list remembering to add everything she'd need for fried chicken and Kane deleted quite a few of her items and added a few others.

"You will eat actual food and I don't want any argument." Yep, stern and very sexy.

She shook her head and was so very tempted to stick her tongue out at him.

Her 'fine' was a bit snippy too.

She asked if he was meeting up with Carl and Warren on Sunday to head back to Bellingham.

"Sweetheart, are you trying to get rid of me already?" His grin told her he was teasing her.

She told him he was welcome to stay with her as long as he'd like but figured he had a business to run.

Becca was thinking about James only coming for a day and a half which meant that she'd have six more days at the cabin once he was gone. She liked her alone time but sort of wanted Kane's company too.

He kissed her hand which brought her back to their present conversation.

"Thank you for that open invitation Becca, it means a lot. I would like to stop by the boat to get some clothes before we head back, if you don't mind." He had his tundra melting smile on.

She was grinning too since clothes meant he was staying for at least another day or two. 'YES!'

Once she stopped jumping up and down inside, she gave him a quick kiss before checking on the drying progress.

He came and helped her fold the sheets. She had the towels and clothes done and in the basket in record time.

Second to last stop… groceries.

She couldn't remember the last time she purchased so much food but now she could at least restock the freezer and Kane again was insisting she eat more. Plus, she did have to buy everything for Sunday's barbeque, and she knew that certain members of her family could eat, a lot.

He'd already crossed off any protein shakes or KIND bars on her list, but she did ask if she could have one or two for backup.

"Real food Becca, you agreed. So, 'NO'." He kind of glared at her.

'Overbearing Jackass.' She gave in with a huge eye roll.

Her appetite was improving with all of their extracurricular activity, but she would still need to watch everything she consumed.

When she went to pay, he stopped her handing the clerk cash. She tried to protest but he put his finger to her lips and told her it was his pleasure.

That was frustrating to her, but she managed a cordial, "Thank you."

Of course, she was thinking, 'Services rendered,' and that made her smile.

She also thought of withholding sex for his highhandedness and over the top generosity.

Oh, who is she kidding.

Final stop was the boat which was down at the City Beach Marina.

She walked with him to keep him company and she liked that he was holding her hand the whole way. They got a few odd looks, but she didn't care. He chose her.

This made her realize that when he did leave, it would wound her heart. Maybe not as deep as other events, but it would hurt like hell.

The boys weren't on board, so it was a quick stop. Kane went and grabbed his duffel bag and put in fresh jeans, a pair of shorts, swim trucks, two shirts, socks, underwear, pajama bottoms, flip-flops and his toiletry bag.

It amazed her how a guy can take so little and be gone for like a week. She would need a suitcase plus a carry on for that same time frame.

"Ready." And with that he reclaimed her hand and headed back to the car.

On the drive back he told her that Carl and Warren could take the boat back on their own and he'd fly to Seattle with her the following Sunday before she headed back to Alaska.

She was 'Miss Perma-grin' at the thought of him staying with her for the rest of her time at the cabin.

She would have been happy with the weekend, this was 'SO MUCH' better.

He also asked how big her bed was in Sitka and if she had room for him to come up for a few weeks over the winter. And would her landlady be okay with that?

He managed to floor her that time.

He went on to shock the living shit out her by asking her to only teach the first semester and come stay with him for the second in Bellingham.

'Fuck, really. That's beyond fast, too fast.' Her thoughts were scattered, and her expression was not quite terror.

"Becca, stop over thinking and just promise me you'll consider it?" He squeezed her hand.

She promised.

He backed the SUV down the hill, which she never did, and they unloaded everything and hauled it down to the cabin. Two trips with all the water jugs.

*Only pain in the ass about their summer retreat. Lake water worked for bathing and dishes, but all drinkable water had to be lugged down the hill.*

*She also wished they had a washer, just for convenience.*

*Her dad liked it a bit more rustic. Hell, he didn't put in power or the septic tank until she was in high school.*

Becca got busy putting everything away.

The fridge looked fully stocked as did the freezer. Mission accomplished.

The sun was making its way down for the evening and she and Kane went out on the top deck to watch all the colors form as it dipped behind the mountains. It was beautiful.

His arms came around her and she leaned back into his chest. "What would you like to do this evening my girl?" His lips were just touching her earlobe.

Very dangerous. It was one of her erogenous zones. She had a few and he found every one of them. More than once.

She pulled away and asked if he wanted to go swimming. He shook his head and pulled her back into his arms.

"You sure, we could go skinny dipping?" Her grin was a tad vengeful.

"Becca, do you think any part of my lower extremities will work in that freezing ass water of yours?" He was smirking.

She shook her head.

She reached up and gave him a swift kiss and asked if he would build a fire. He nodded but not before giving her a much more intimate kiss.

Yeah… sex was back on the table again, with a vengeance.

While Kane was making the fire, Becca went and remade the king-sized bed with fresh sheets. She had just pulled the bedspread on when he was behind her.

"Need help Beautiful?" Then he reached down and pulled the bedspread back along with the light blanket and top sheet.

Her body was alive as she shuddered from his touch.

"I love that you want me as much as I want you." And he helped get her undressed.

She was laying in his arms again, thinking 'So much for clean sheets but so much fun fucking them up again.' And chuckled to herself

"What is so funny?" When she told him, he rolled her over and gave her a quick slap on the ass.

"You know I find that arousing, right?" She gave him her own devious grin.

With a knowing wink he gave her three harder smacks and followed it up with a rather spectacular orgasm.

Again, his stamina was quite voracious.

She cooked him a late dinner that night and did eat the chicken stir fry as promised. But he got all the fried rice.

After cleaning up the kitchen and while Kane was otherwise pre-occupied, she took the opportunity for a quick dip in her lake.

Her body was enjoying the cool water, especially her lady parts which were, as I'm sure you could only imagine, sore. She was again lost in her own thoughts when he spoke, and she gasped in surprise.

He had an uncanny way of sneaking up on her.

"Becca, you know I have an issue with water and you swimming at night alone, makes me crazy. So, I'd like for you to come out now." His voice was rather stern.

She shook her head and suggested he join her.

"Not tonight. And I'm very serious, I want you out, now." He was getting upset so she swam up to the dock and informed him she was standing on the rocks. It wasn't that deep and to please stop worrying about her.

That seemed to calm him, but just.

She tried to lighten his mood by splashing him, but he wasn't amused.

To somewhat appease her over protective fella, she continued her swim very close to shore.

When he turned and headed back to the cabin, she ducked underwater and swam for the back of the dock and emerged at the ladder. She loved playing with her lake.

Oh, yeah… that freaked him the fuck out.

She climbed up and found Kane standing there with her towel looking more than a little upset.

After she wrapped the towel around herself, Kane pulled her into a huge bear hug. Becca could feel his heart racing. He was scared for her.

She felt bad and told him that the lake wouldn't harm her, and he didn't need to worry. She also told him how sorry she was for frightening him.

His look was harsh with an undertone of hurt when he finally let her go and headed back to the cabin without taking her hand.

She was deep in thought as she watched him head into the cabin. 'How am I going to make him understand how important my lake is to me?' She decided to sit on the dock for a few minutes to let him cool down.

Becca hated stressful situations; she had had her share. Enough for one lifetime actually but she also really liked Kane and wanted him to stick around.

But was she willing to give up part of who she was for someone else?

She did that before and it almost killed her.

Decision made, take baby steps regarding the lake and she headed up to dry off; the night air was giving her a slight chill.

She found him watching TV when she came back inside, and he didn't even look up to acknowledge her.

'Yep, still pissed'. She sighed.

She grabbed a pair of shorts and T-shirt and headed into the bathroom.

She decided it would be smart to blow dry her wet hair before putting on her sleeping attire.

In his mood she knew sex wasn't going to be an issue and since she was still very sore from yesterday and again today, she really just wanted to cuddle.

As an olive branch of sorts Becca grabbed them both a water and went and sat by him on the couch.

He refused the water with a single shake of his head and still wouldn't make eye contact.

She wasn't just getting a chill sitting next to him, it was Arctic cold. She was amazed she didn't get frostbite.

'I am too fucking old for this shit.' And with that internal thought she decided to head for bed and try to read.

Kane came in over an hour later and changed into his pajama bottoms and got in on the other side without so much as a good night or 'fuck off'.

Becca reached over and touched his shoulder not wanting him to go to bed angry with her and he pushed her hand away.

That hurt her more than him yelling at her. Or even hitting her.

Her heart seized.

Sometimes a king-sized bed just isn't big enough.

She waited for him to fall asleep and went out into the living room and slept on the couch.

Sleep being relative; her mind was wide awake.

She so wished she could call Mary and talk to her about Kane. Her late best friend was brilliant at giving advice when it came to relationships and that made Becca's heart hurt even more than Kane's rejection. She missed her friend so very much.

Looking around the cabin made her realize how much she missed her mom as well.

The tears came quick, and she wanted a hug.

Her dad gave great hugs. She wanted him to hold her like he did when she was little after a bad dream.

'Reality Bites.' Dinner got flushed a few moments later.

Back on the couch, Becca wrapped her arms around her knees and sobbed quietly in the dark.

With the loss of both parents and Mary her heart didn't break but created deep fissures, and they never seemed to completely heal. This night the fractures were working overtime and she felt so very alone.

His arms coming around her startled her and intensified her tears. He wrapped her up in his embrace and stroked her hair and kissed her forehead.

He never spoke one word. He just kept her in his arms. This made her feel better and after a bit of time the tears stopped, and she started shaking from the night chill and all the emotional release.

She needed to let him go. He was becoming so very important to her. Her heart couldn't take another crevice. That might push her over the edge into utter despair, a place she'd been only once before and had no desire to return.

He took her hand and led her into the bedroom and cradled her back in his arms. "Sleep, my darling girl." And gave her a very tender kiss.

# SATURDAY

Becca woke before six. Kane was still fast asleep.

She really needed to thank him for his kindness.

She would also let him know that he didn't cause last night's episode... well not entirely.

And then let him get on with his life... she wondered if she had that kind of selflessness within her.

He was young enough to still have a family.

Decision made. Her adoration for him meant she needed to tell him to leave.

But right now, she needed to change her focus.

With her brother's arrival later in the day, she got up and decided to get the cabin cleaned up.

She started in the bathroom since that was her first stop anyway. She then got the fire going and dusted and tidied the living room. She would wait to vacuum since it was a bit noisy.

After getting coffee made, she swept and mopped the kitchen floor all before Kane was even awake.

She would need to go and make the bed in the bunkhouse and sweep the upper deck and maybe wash the windows. But first she needed caffeine.

She snuck into the bedroom and grabbed her testing kit.

He was still deep in sleep.

She smiled at the lovely man in her bed.

'Can I really let him go?' She shook her head.

After testing, she wrote down her fasting number in her ledger and got her first cup of coffee.

It was just after seven, so she ventured down to the dock.

She loved this time of the day, so quiet… It wouldn't stay that way. The lake was always crazy on weekends.

An eagle made an appearance that morning… probably looking for its first meal of the day.

She really did love the cabin.

It offered such tranquility.

Kane was coming down the dock with his own cup of coffee and she took that moment to enjoy that incredible view.

He was wearing his pajama bottoms and an open flannel shirt that revealed his lovely chest hair. 'OH MY.'

He bent down and gave her a very nice good morning kiss.

"Hello Beautiful, you've been busy this morning. The cabin looks spotless. When did you get up?" He took the chair next to hers and intertwined her fingers with his.

"Around six. James is more anal than I am in regard to cleanliness, so I do try to placate him since we don't see each other very often. You two would probably get along fine. But I think we need to talk." Her look was apprehensive.

"Becca, I'm sorry for being an ass about you swimming last night. If you'll bear with me, I'll try and calm my phobia. I never want to make you sad again. And I think maybe you've been over thinking this morning since it sounds like you're about to give me my walking papers. Please don't say you want me to go. Because all I want to do is stay and take you back to bed." His look took her by surprise.

It wasn't just a hopeful expression but one of sheer adulation.

She smiled at him and thought she must have done something good in a past life to warrant this wonderful sexy man's affection.

"I am very confused about my feelings and part of me thinks you deserve to find someone to start a family with, to grow old with. But in saying that I think I'd forever miss you." A single tear escaped her eye.

He had her up and into his arms. "Becca, if I wanted kids, I think I might have started my family years ago. And I would be honored to grow old with you. Please let me stay." He leaned and kissed away her tear.

She almost gasped at that loving statement. "If you really want to stay, can we make a pact?"

He pulled away to look at her and nodded.

"I promise to stay closer to shore if I swim at night if you promise never to push me away again." Her voice cracked at the end.

She was remembering how much that hurt and her eyes glistened, but no tears fell that time.

He wrapped his arms around her tighter.

"Oh, my sweet woman, it's a deal. I never want to cause you that kind of pain again. Please forgive me." She melted into his hug.

Damn she was really beginning to develop deep feelings for this man.

His lips were playing with her ear. "Becca sweetheart, I'm going to take you back to bed now." When his tongue joined the party all she could do was moan.

Moments later he was showing her how much he cherished her.

Again.

She was feeling quite loved and enjoying just lying there and caressing his gorgeously firm ass for a change. He told her it felt amazing but if she wanted to get the bunkhouse ready for her brother, she'd better stop.

She didn't... She even bent down and bit his delectable tush followed by a tender kiss.

"Damn you woman." And he had her pinned.

They both were beyond spent after that escapade and, truth was, she was very proud of herself, and her body quite enjoyed it as well.

After a bit of cuddling, she got up and fixed him a hearty breakfast with ham, hash browns, eggs and toast.

He ate every bite. She managed two eggs and a small piece of ham.

*No, she didn't tell him that she threw up dinner. Would you?*

Kane offered to do the dishes so she could finish cleaning the cabin. A quick vacuum and then outside to sweep the porch and wash all the windows she could reach.

The ones in the living room required a fifteen-foot ladder. She'd let her nephew Jake do the high windows since heights and she didn't exactly like each other.

Once done with the outside she moved inside to clean those as well, again minus the panes she couldn't reach.

Now all she needed to do was grab the bedding for the bunkhouse.

Kane had made their bed and was sitting on it when she came in to get the linens.

He was looking guilty, and she asked what was wrong.

"I've invaded your privacy." He looked almost ashamed.

She smirked.

"My dear man, you've invaded much of me these past couple days, privacy seems small in comparison."

He raised his eyebrows and winked at her.

"I read your testing numbers — they seem low — why haven't you talked to me about your diabetes?" His look was both loving and concerned.

She hated talking about her disease and about the only one that ever got away with it was Mary... and only because she was there when Becca found out she had it.

PLUS, Mary was a force, and you really didn't get much of a choice when she set her mind to something. *Sound familiar?*

With a tad too much sarcasm she said, "When? Between, 'Oh baby yes! yes! yes!' to hey, how about we chat about my hemoglobin A1C."

"Rebecca Lynne, so help me God... I'm about to put you over my knee and it won't be arousing. I am trying to have a serious conversation with you. Your health matters to me. You matter." He raised his voice a bit there at the end.

He knew she didn't like him to use her full name and was thinking of walking out, but she didn't want to fight with him any more. She almost called him Christian to see if he'd get the reference but thought better of it.

She sat next to him on the bed. "Kane, I hate talking about my numbers with anyone. If you want to look at my ledger, feel free... anytime. And you're right, a few days were a tad low but as long as they stay above seventy-five when fasting, I don't have to worry too much about crashing. And I'm glad I matter. You matter to me as well." And with that she stood up and gathered up the linens.

He pulled her back onto the bed displacing the sheets on the floor.

He had his lips to her ear and was exploring with his tongue. She moaned and pulled his lips back to hers with a very passionate kiss.

Her body was in full want mode.

Damn!

He stopped their kiss and got off the bed and picked up the bedding asking if she needed help getting the guest quarters ready.

'Fuck, really.'

She was pissed at him for teasing her wide-awake libido. The one he created after all.

She glared at him and grabbed the bundle with a bit of force and told him, "I. Do. Not!"

He was chuckling as he followed her down the beach. 'Jackass.'

She was making the bed and screamed, bringing Kane running inside the small guest quarters.

It was this day he found out she was terrified of spiders.

Being quite gallant he took care of the eight-legged intruder and helped Becca finish making the bed.

She thought about kissing him but changed her mind and did a verbal, 'thank you,' instead.

"What, no kiss for vanquishing the evil entity?" He was so teasing her.

She was still miffed about the fake foreplay, so she just shook her head.

Still a few hours before her big brother's arrival, she made the decision to calm her libido and give him a bit of payback in the process.

She went and put on her swimsuit and, without so much as a, 'Kiss my ass,' walked down the dock and dove off the end.

She started swimming out about twenty or so feet.

Kane was standing there watching her. His expression wasn't quite panic, but it was close.

Well shit, she didn't want to upset him that much, even if he liked messing with her.

As she was thinking, she was swimming back towards the dock but didn't go to the ladder. She swam towards the shallower depths closer to the shoreline and could see him instantly calm down.

"Becca, please don't swim out that far again. I know I said I'd work on my fear, but could you help a little?" His face was almost pleading.

She nodded.

After all she had a phobia about spiders, and he didn't try and throw one at her.

'Good analogy Becs.'

She saw the sheriff's boat coming so she went and climbed out at the shore.

Once wrapped in her towel, she gave Kane an 'I'm sorry kiss' and went to greet her nephew.

He took her hand as the boat approached.

"Hey JJ. Your pops won't be here for another three or four hours." She was smiling at Jake's expression of her new guy.

"This is Curtis Kane. I apologize for not introducing you the other day."

The boat came alongside the dock and Jake reached out to shake Kane's hand... which made him drop Becca's.

"Nice to meet you Mr Kane. This is my partner, Justin Grant." How formal she thought.

They just nodded at each other.

She was about to laugh at the testosterone being displayed. The only thing missing was showing penile erections.

'What idiots.'

"What do you two want?" She gave her nephew and his partner an evil smile.

In unison. "Nothing." And with a, 'Nice to meet you and see you later,' they took off.

Kane looked back at her and she smiled. "My family, love 'em and still want to beat the living crap out of them."

"Yeah, wait until you meet mine." He winked at her.

"So, how about I make up for my early faux pas in the bedroom?"

She shook her head.

"That time has passed Curt. Best of the luck next time."

"Oh sweetheart, luck has nothing to do with it. Are you actually trying to play hard to get?" His grin was wicked.

Seriously having another déjà vu moment.

Freaky Fucking Saturday.

"Becca, I know when you're thinking the word too. And that counts."

She stuck her tongue out at him.

Taking a step back with the plan of jumping in the lake, he picked up on that and pulled her into a very passionate kiss.

Yep, her body was a traitor and gave into its lustful desires.

And don't think he didn't take full advantage.

After her very powerful orgasm, she looked up and playfully asked if he'd like to discuss her diabetes now?

That got a rather good slap on her ass.

"Guess not." And she laughed.

Yep… Another slap and it was a bit harder. But he caressed it after, and she nestled into his embrace.

She fell back to sleep and was surprised the clock read twelve forty-five when she woke.

Kane was watching her.

"Good afternoon Beautiful. You were sleeping so soundly I didn't want to wake you." And he gave her a very nice kiss.

She looked him in the eye. "I seriously adore you Kane." And with that declaration she got up and grabbed her robe.

He was up and had her back in his arms and putting his lips to her ear. "I feel the same way."

She was beginning to fall in love with this amazing man and it sort of scared her.

She needed to refocus her thoughts on another task.

Becca told him he could have the shower first.

While Kane was busy it was the perfect time to make her brother's favorite smoked salmon dip.

She had hidden the salmon from all prying eyes just for this occasion.

*Douglas, her landlady's son, had a subsistence license and was very good at getting his quota of sockeye salmon each year. He also had an amazing way of smoking it and was incredibly generous in sharing it... something Becca appreciated very much.*

She had the mixture done when Kane came out in jeans... so 'fucking' sexy.

WOOF!

"That looks good, what is it?"

She put some on a cracker and fed him the dip.

"Damn, smoked salmon dip. You made that? Best I've ever tasted."

She grinned and put it in the fridge to chill.

Before heading into the shower, she handed him the sandwich she'd made him and a bag of chips. She also let him know as soon as her brother was settled, she'd bring the dip back out, but he would have to hurry if he wanted any since there were never leftovers.

Her brother could eat.

He gave her, her favorite grin, along with a very nice thank you kiss.

It's strange how the mind works.

While showering she remembered another sandwich… this one… her ex was eating.

*For some reason that day she was trying to make an effort enticing him back into their bedroom.*

*Maybe getting their love life back on track. It was, of course, much earlier in their marriage. Before his alcoholism got totally out of hand.*

*When she asked him to join her in their bedroom, he told her that he'd rather just eat… it was the last time she ever asked. That odd memory used to make her sad now it just pissed her off.*

*I really should have divorced his ass ten years sooner.*

Woulda! Coulda! Shoulda!

She emerged from the bathroom in a towel and another one on her head, leaving more of her ugly past behind her.

He pinned her against the wall by the kitchen entrance with a very powerful kiss and opened her towel for access to her breasts. His fingers explored her arousal. He leaned into her ear and told her he wanted her to think of him inside her for the rest of the day and ended this sensual attack by licking his fingers and retying her towel.

She caught her breath and slowed her heart before heading back to the bedroom. 'FUCK!'

'Paybacks are coming Kane,' she thought and needed to find a way to get him aroused. Frustratingly aroused.

BINGO!

She found her mom's little frilly apron... little being the keyword.

It was stark white with lace around the top and bottom and just covered the breasts and barely went to the top of her thighs. It was perfect.

She towel-dried her hair into her version of 'the sexy but unkempt look' and put on the little apron. Well, what there was of an apron.

'This is going to take timing.' She was trying not to over think especially about why her mother had that damn thing in the first place.

'Oh, hell no, don't go there.'

Back on track... get even with Kane.

She stood in the door frame of the bedroom with her hand on the door and asked him if fried chicken sounded good for dinner.

When he looked around from the couch his eyes nearly bugged out of his head, and he actually growled at her.

He was quicker than she thought he'd be, but she still managed to shut and lock the door before he got to it.

She laughed her most sinister laugh and had a huge smile on her face as she took off the apron and put on her comfy boy short underwear and jeans.

He was banging pretty hard. She hoped the door would hold.

"Becca, open this fucking door right now. You don't get to wear that and not give me access." He was aroused.

'Good!'

She was very pleased with her payback and buttoned up her shirt, put on her sandals and headed out the back door that led around the side of the cabin and down to the beach.

When her dad built the new bedroom, he added another room, which she thought was eventually supposed to be a private en suite for he and her mom but it ended up as a catch all room, but today the back door he installed came in handy since Kane was still banging on the main bedroom door.

She yelled at the door he was still pounding on, "Paybacks are a bitch Kane." And with that, she locked the storage door before she made her get away.

The 'JJ's' were back and that made her smile since it should calm Kane down. She also heard the truck on the hill. 'Perfect timing gentlemen.'

"Hey, Jake, your dad appears to be at the top of the hill. You both staying to say 'hi'?" She grabbed the rope he tossed.

That would be a yes.

She was tying up the boat when Justin asked where Kane was going.

She looked back and he was shaking his head at her while heading around to the back of the cabin where she just exited from.

She lost any future escape routes.

'Well shit.'

She shrugged.

"Aunt Becs… what the hell is up with your hair? Bit wild for you?"

She loved embarrassing her nephew.

"SEX will do that." And winked.

Whatever Justin was drinking at the time sprayed all over the boat and Jake.

She got the giggles.

Jake was blushing and looking pissed at his friend and partner.

Becca had just reached the upper deck when Kane was coming back out the main door. The bedroom door now wide open.

He leaned into her. "You are in so much trouble." And gave her a very evil grin.

She reminded him, he started it.

"I'm going to finish it too, sweetheart, you just wait." And turned and walked down to the dock.

That threat was quite arousing.

'FUCK ME!'

She managed to get a brush through her hair before James came in the back door.

Huge bear hug from her brother.

"Damn I've missed you sis. You need to come spend a week or two with me in Billings next summer. You look great by the way."

"Thank you. Miss you too James and when are you going to come up to Alaska for a little halibut fishing. You've been promising that for a few years now." He nodded and shrugged.

Jake was next to give his dad a big hug. James asked him why his shirt was wet.

His response of, 'Boat spray,' made Becca laugh, again.

Justin gave James a hug too… he might as well be the third son.

Kane was standing back, and Becca grabbed his hand and brought him to meet her big brother.

The two shook hands and made polite conversation.

"Jake, why don't you take your dad's bag down to the bunkhouse for him." She then asked if anyone was hungry and they all were, even Kane.

No surprise there.

Kane helped her get the dip and crackers out and she cut up some meat and cheese to add to the assortment.

She also gave him a kiss and thanked him for being there.

His mood improved immensely.

With snacks served, her brother went and got his cooler off the back porch. He did like his beer and knew she wouldn't buy him any.

He didn't go crazy, but she had a rule about not buying alcohol for anyone.

*She was accused of being an enabler to her husband when he drank and that pissed her off to no end.*

*Her ex would badger her, yell at her and call her every name in the book until she'd finally give in and would go and get his booze.*

'Mother Fucker.'

She shook her head to get back into the here and now.

Kane was watching her closely.

"So, James have you heard from Mark? Are they bringing the kids out tomorrow for the barbeque? I haven't heard a word from him since I got here."

Her brother shrugged his shoulders. He stopped making excuses for his eldest son many years prior. It wasn't worth the effort. That and he'd be apologizing every time he and Becca spoke.

"I cannot believe she is still holding some arbitrary grudge against me!" Becs was looking a tad miffed since she really liked spending time with Mark and the kids but never got to see him since his 'fucking' wife had a problem with her. A problem that no one would ever tell her how to fix.

James changed the subject and asked Kane if he'd like a beer.

Jake returned from his errand down the beach and grabbed a cracker for some dip and asked his aunt if she'd like a swim before he had to get back to work.

He knew she had an issue with drinking.

She smiled at her very sweet and observant nephew. Also noting that she'd need to make a double batch of dip the next time since the men made short work of finishing it off in record time. Even for them.

As stated before, they could eat.

Jake raised his eyebrow waiting for her response.

He really was her favorite.

She nodded and got up to change.

Kane followed her out onto the upper deck where she retrieved her suit.

"Becca, what's up? Your whole body is tense, and you look almost pale." He had her in his arms.

"Do you drink?" She was afraid of his answer.

"Sure, on occasion. Few beers now and then. Watching a game usually. A glass of wine with a nice dinner maybe. But I've not been drunk since I was in my early twenties. If it bothers you, I don't need a beer."

He pulled her face up to look at him.

"No, you should have a beer with James. I want you two to get to know each other. It's not a big thing. Do you mind me swimming?" She thought it only fair since he asked her permission, of sorts.

He shook his head and told her to go have fun with Jake.

She brought his lips to hers and gave him a rather intimate kiss.

"You just wait until later sweetheart." He slapped her ass and went back inside.

She was glad that part of the deck couldn't be seen from the living room.

She was blushing when she made her way into the bedroom to change.

She again went out the back door, down to the dock and jumped into the cool lake water.

Jack came out of the cabin and ran down the dock and dove in to join her.

"So, Jake, what is the deal with your brother's wife? It's been going on for years and I'm beyond over it." She decided to quiz him out of his father's earshot hoping he might have a clue. She'd asked oodles of times the past several years.

"Aunt Becs, I really don't know. She doesn't like me much either. She's a bit of a goody-goody. I don't understand what Mark sees in her. Except her huge tits." He was smiling.

Becca was a bit shocked at her nephew's thoughts on his sister-in-law's attributes.

"She seems to like your dad just fine."

He shook his head.

"She's not stupid. She'd ever say anything against Pops or Mark would be gone and he'd fight her for the kids."

Wow that again was a bit of a surprise to her.

*James raised the boys since Mark was six and Jake was four. His second wife, Laura, decided she didn't like being a mother and one day packed up and was gone. Bitch!*

*His first wife, Shelia, was a high school sweetheart and that only lasted about a year and a half. Becca referred to that as, 'His trial by fire marriage'. Hell, it was over and done with before she was even in high school.*

*James' third wife, Rhonda, was very sweet and made a great surrogate mom for the boys but, when James moved his company to Montana, she didn't go.*

*He never found number four, probably for the best considering his track record.*

*He had more than enough women who liked spending time with him.*

*At least that's what he always told her.*

*Truth was, her brother was a bit of a hound dog.*

*Still, she loved the shit out of him.*

*They were polar opposites. She was liberal, could be mouthy, and tried to keep her marriage together through a lot of turmoil, some that caused her great pain.*

*He was conservative, chose his words carefully, hated conflict and had sex with anything that stood still long enough.*

*Losing their folks is what brought them back together.*

*She was sure her mom and dad were happy about that.*

"Earth to Becca? Come in Aunt Becs." Jake splashed his aunt in the face with enough lake water she choked.

That brought her out of her head, and she went under water, found his legs and pulled him under. 'Little shit.'

She then swam to the ladder and climbed up on the dock. To her surprise Kane was there with a towel.

"Hi Beautiful, have a good swim?" He wrapped her up in the towel and in his arms.

She didn't want to get him wet and tried to pull away and he was having none of that.

She hugged him back and got a very nice kiss.

When Jake came up the ladder, he told them to get a room.

His playful aunt pushed him off the dock and back into the lake.

About that same time, Justin called down and told Jake to stop messing around they had a call out.

Break time was officially over.

Back on the dock, he grabbed his towel wrapped it around his waist and removed his swim trucks tossing them at his aunt.

"Hang those up for me please. I'll get them tomorrow. Thanks Aunt Becs, love you." He flashed her as he ran into the cabin. She couldn't help but laugh.

Damn she loved that boy.

"Where is James?" she asked, looking back at Kane.

"He was on the phone and started to yell at someone, so I made myself scarce." He shrugged.

She nodded and they both took seats on the dock.

He never let go of her hand.

It was a small gesture but one that she adored him for.

The boys came racing down and she got a quick peck on the cheek from Jake and, 'See you tomorrow,' as Justin untied their boat. Once started they were off like a bat out of hell.

She just shook her head.

James came down a few minutes later with a water in his hand and told her that plans had changed, and he was sorry, but they wouldn't get as long a visit as he hoped for.

"What's up?" She was a bit disappointed and a little more than curious.

"Mark is taking the kids to 'Silverwood' tomorrow and told them that Grandpa would be coming too. So, I'll be taking off after breakfast and won't be back until dinner most likely."

*'Silverwood' is an amusement park just outside of Athol, Idaho. In case you were wondering.*

She was now extremely pissed off at Mark since he knew she wasn't down for more than a few weeks. And he hadn't even bothered to call or bring the kids to see her.

"He's out of my will. I'm leaving everything to the 'Coalition for a Better Yesterday'."

Kane chuckled at that remark. Her brother just shook his head.

"Will you still fix me mom's fried chicken for dinner?" James was pouting.

She rolled her eyes and nodded.

"Thanks sis. I'm going to lay down for a bit. That drive gets harder each time. It sucks to get old."

And with that he started for the bunkhouse.

Becca yelled when he got halfway there. "You could retire you know."

He just waved.

She smiled and noticed that Kane's look was a tad seductive.

She was, in fact, not in the mood. She wanted to plot some revenge on her eldest nephew. 'Jackass.'

His eyebrow went up and he pulled her into his waiting lips.

Holy Hell!

"Let's see about getting you out of that wet swimsuit and into a nice dry bed, shall we."

All thoughts of paybacks were gone.

Those damn lips of his were lethal.

"Yes please."

He liked that statement and pulled her into another passionate kiss before they even made it off the dock.

She felt his erection and took his hand as they went up the back way to their room.

After shutting and locking the door she made quick work of getting naked and he made short work of relieving both their sexual tensions.

Once they had both caught their breath, he pulled the apron she had on early out from under his pillow.

"Put it one, now." He was almost growling again.

She did as she was told.

His tongue was all over her breasts, pulling them out from under the garment. Once suitably hard he put them back where they belonged and moved to his lower target.

He was driving her crazy and she tried to move. He held her legs and shook his head letting her know to stop moving.

She was on the verge of climaxing, and he stopped.

Before she could beg him to continue his tongue continued its rhythm and again, he stopped before she came. He did it once more before he let her have her orgasm. She ended up having several aftershocks and right when she thought he was done, he slid back inside her for his own powerful release.

'Fuck, he really is going to kill me,' was her only thought as she shut her eyes and fell asleep.

Kane was giving her kisses and telling her it was time to get up. Her brother would be over soon, and they needed to get dinner going.

She stirred and looked into those amazing green eyes.

"Please tell me you're real. I couldn't bear this being a dream."

He pinched her ass, hard. "Ouch."

"Not a dream Becca. I'm here and I'm all yours."

Her tears caught him by surprise.

"I dreamt of you. You're my ultimate fantasy coming true." She gave him a kiss.

He wiped her tears away.

"Sweetheart, I may not have dreamt of you, but you are a dream come true for me as well."

Damn she loved that smile.

His lips parted hers and they had a very intimate interlude before getting out of bed.

No orgasm.

So much better.

They were falling in love.

She had dinner well in hand by the time her brother resurfaced from his afternoon slumber.

She was doubly glad that he was tired from his drive. It gave her a very nice late afternoon tryst in bed with Kane.

The chicken was getting its fry on, potatoes were almost ready to mash, and she had biscuits in the oven.

She forgot the corn on the cob, so he'd have to live with a garden salad for his vegetable. It was the only thing on the menu that night Becca was willing to eat.

She threw a chicken breast in the oven to bake so neither her brother nor Kane would have some hissy fit about her not eating enough.

It was bad enough with one getting on her case... she had two.

Once dinner was served the boys chowed down and she enjoyed watching them both eat the dinner she prepared.

She managed half of the chicken breast with her salad and neither of them said a word.

James gave her kudos for the great chicken, Kane concurred.

The conversation was mainly focused on the next day's barbeque and his upcoming trek to the amusement park. He also told her how sorry he was again for messing up the plans and for the way his eldest son was acting.

Apparently, he called Mark back once he woke and told him that it was rude to ignore his only aunt and why hadn't he invited her as well as Jake to the park.

His response of 'Amy' fueled her brother's anger, but he also wanted to spend time with his three grandchildren, Ashley, Collin and baby Gail. Who was actually five now, so baby was just her placement in the family line.

Mark also informed his dad that they were going the day prior but when he had to postpone his arrival by one day due to the planning commission meeting, they moved their day at the park to accommodate him coming over from Montana since the kids wanted their grandpa to join them for the day. That lessened James' ire but not Becca's. Still, she knew she'd have to let it go. Eventually!

She told him to stop worrying about it. She didn't much like amusement parks and, as stated earlier, Amy didn't like her.

'Feeling is mutual, you fucking bitch.' Again, snarky in thought only but still, a little anger management might be in order.

Kane squeezed her hand and shook his head.

How did he know she dropped the 'f' bomb in her head?

She again stuck her tongue out at him and started to clear the table.

With such a small kitchen, she told both men to go into the living room and watch TV while she cleaned up; but did ask if either one would like coffee. They both declined.

"You cooked sis I should clean up?" His look was more, 'Please don't take me up on the offer I'm just being nice.'

She shook her head and could tell he was relieved.

Kane did stay and tried to help, but once he realized he was more in the way, he gave her a quick kiss and went and joined James in the other room.

"Smart man. She'll kick you out eventually for being underfoot." He offered Kane another beer but was told, No thanks.

Becca was beyond thrilled by that.

Kane was the only man who ever had sex with her sober. It meant more than she'd ever be able to express to him.

*But since he didn't actually know that information, mum's the word.*

"So, how long have you been sleeping with my sister?" Big brothers can be such a pain in the ass.

He didn't see the soapy sponge until it hit him in the head.

"What the hell Becs?"

She came and retrieved the sponge and put her finger to her lips with a 'shush'.

"So, not long. Treat her right or you'll be killed." He had a big brother evil grin on his face.

Kane not backing down one bit was quick to reply.

"I wouldn't dare hurt your sister. I happen to adore her very much."

'AWE! Ditto!' Her insides were feeling warm.

'I'll tell James tomorrow how much I care for Kane, that should calm his worry.'

James nodded his approval of that statement.

She finished up with the kitchen smiling the whole time.

But now she felt sticky… some from their earlier afternoon delight since she didn't have time to shower before she started cooking and, of course, frying chicken made her feel sort of gross.

She headed to the bedroom and put on her other swim suit and headed down for a dip.

Kane went with her.

As promised, she stayed closer to shore and he stayed fairly calm through the whole ordeal.

"Would you like to come and join me? I'd like for you and my lake to become friends." She was hoping he would.

"Maybe tomorrow. Right now, I just want to watch you." His look was so very sweet and less stressed.

She nodded and swam for a few more minutes before the chill got to even her.

He wrapped her up in the towel and his arms giving her a very tender kiss.

"Kane, since we've had copious amounts of sex the past few days, would you mind if tonight we just cuddle." She didn't want to offend him, but she was still sore... quite sore.

"That sounds perfect actually. I'd like to discuss tomorrow with you and perhaps an outing for Monday after your brother heads for home." She loved that smile. And nodded.

Back inside she put on her two-piece pajama set that she got from a friend three birthdays ago, a bit too big now but so very comfy. She hung her suit and towel on the front porch railing and grinned.

*Her dad hated that, he put the clothes line in the back of the cabin so no one would 'display their wares and disturb his view'... James came by his anal attitude naturally.*

'Sorry dad, but it's so much more convenient.' She smirked at the thought.

She was surprised when her phone rang, no one called her that often and at quarter after ten at night was unheard of.

"Hello." She knew it was an Alaskan number but didn't recognize it.

"Hi Douglas. I'm sorry, you're where?" It was very noisy on his end.

"NO! When?" Her eyes glistened as the tears formed.

"Yes, of course… no I have one… sure… I appreciate you letting me know and I'm so very sorry for your loss."

And the call ended.

Becca just made it into the bathroom before she threw up dinner for the second night in a row.

"Becca are you okay? What's going on? Can I please come in?" Kane saw her face, but she was already in the bathroom by the time he was in motion.

She answered from the other side of the door. "Clara died. I need a minute please." She started crying.

He opened the door and pulled her into his arms.

She was afraid she might throw up again, but he wasn't going to let her stay on the bathroom floor and almost carried her into the bedroom and cradled her in his arms letting her tears soak into his shirt, again for the second night in a row.

*James, if you're wondering, was passed out cold on the couch. Long day of driving, huge dinner and two and a half beers. Lightweight.*

Kane held Becca for the rest of the night. She cried herself to sleep in his arms.

# SUNDAY

The clock read five a.m. and her head was pounding. She'd need to get up soon and test her numbers.

Becca was still feeling the loss of her dear friend and landlady and at that exact moment in time didn't much care to do anything at all.

Kane must have sensed she was awake since his arms pulled her close and he kissed her cheek.

There were no more tears, just a sadness and another small fissure in her heart.

"Becca, I am so sorry about Clara. Is there anything I can do? Would you like to fly back today? I'd be happy to go with you." He was rubbing her back.

How could one man be so wonderful, so caring, so loving, how did she get this lucky at her age to find him? Well, he found her. But still.

She was feeling very blessed.

"Thank you… but no. I'll leave as intended, a week from today." She turned and gave him a tender kiss.

She got up and grabbed her testing kit and went out to put on a pot of coffee.

She also wanted to check on her brother since her night had taken a depressing turn.

He was gone. Must have decided to head down to the bunkhouse sometime during the night. More comfortable that's for sure.

The couch wasn't full size but did pull out into a twin bed when needed.

Of course, you would have to rearrange the entire living room to make that happen. So, it didn't happen very often.

Kane was making the fire when she came out of the bathroom.

She'd washed her face and got her hair a bit more under control. Her eyes were only a little puffy from crying.

She stopped and let Kane give her another hug and lead her to the kitchen table. "I want to know what your numbers are Becca. Please check them. You don't look right."

She loved that he cared so much.

It usually drove her nuts… not today.

She tested low… really low and she had no desire to eat so it was a bad situation.

Kane found her last protein drink in the back of the fridge and handed it to her.

"Drink this please. It's a start at least and then you can have your coffee." His smile was lovely.

She did as he requested.

Becca thanked him for his kindness, but her eyes were still full of utter sorrow.

"Sweetheart, please I want to help. Just tell me how." He had her hands in his.

"You are, just by being here. I need nothing more than time to grieve."

Not her first rodeo with losing someone.

She loved him but was so afraid of the emotion since it would hurt like hell when he left. Another fissure. She brought his hand to her lips and kissed his open palm. And then began talking to him.

"When Mom got sick, we moved down to Nevada, closer to where Mary was living. Well in the same state. The ex-needed a warmer climate for health reasons, and I needed to be able to travel to see my folks more. I hated leaving Alaska. I had a great paying job in Juneau, but you do what's necessary for family. So, we sold the house, got a little two-bedroom modular for cheap and with the extra funds from selling the Alaska property, I didn't have to work right away and that made my travels to northern Idaho a lot easier. Usually alone since my husband was having his own issues. Not life threatening by any means, but he had his own issues to deal with and walking and sitting for long periods were difficult for him." She took a drink of her coffee and continued.

"Mom didn't respond to the chemo like the doctors hoped and she opted out of the program to enjoy her last summer here at the cabin. Dad couldn't handle her being in any kind of pain, so he put her back in the hospital, which she didn't want, but it's what he needed for her. And being the ever-dutiful wife, she let him have his way. She died shortly after." Her eyes were glistening with unshed tears.

"Dad and James had just gone down for some coffee so it was just me, by myself, watching my mom take her last breath." Kane moved closer to hold her as the tears made their way down her cheeks.

"I came back a few times to check on Dad and once to spread mom's ashes in the upper meadow and we put some in the lake as well. She wanted to be with both her parents." She took a short pause.

"I was back in Nevada when Jake called to tell me my dad died. It was a shock actually since he wasn't ill as far as any of us knew. I think that's why James and I also figured he died from a broken heart. Anyway, I came back a month or so later to help with packing, cleaning and selling their house."

"My brother and I were left a nice inheritance, which included this cabin. We waited until the following summer to spread Dad's ashes with Mom's in the meadow." He kissed her forehead when she paused her story.

She smiled at him, but it didn't touch her eyes.

"Mary helped me through the loss the best she could. She'd call me every day to see how I was holding up. Some days she'd just let me cry. One day she told me that I needed to get on with my life and convinced me to get back to work. My marriage was on the rocks then anyway, so I decided to look for a job back in Alaska even though I knew I'd be going alone. I was more than alone anyway." She stopped again and went to refill her coffee and grab a tissue.

While she was up, she turned on the oven since her brother would be joining them soon enough and she had to get breakfast on the table.

Kane shook his head, marveling at her multitasking.

She sat back down and waited for him to put his arm back around her.

"When I made inquiries about jobs, a colleague suggested teaching a marketing course utilizing my twenty-five-plus years' experience. I made contact with the local university in Juneau, and they didn't have an opening, but Sitka did, so I applied. And to my surprise, I got the gig. I did ask the ex if he wanted to go back with me and he said no but told me he didn't want a divorce either. Probably since I'd been the breadwinner for over a decade by then." She took another drink of coffee.

"So, for the first two years I spent forty weeks north and twelve weeks south. I remember being so scared on my first day of class but to my surprise it turned out to be quite entertaining. I even astounded myself, I was pretty good at it." She paused as Kane kissed her cheek.

"Of course, it pays crap, but the insurance is great, and I only work twenty hours a week in four, ten-week intervals and get summers off which I very much enjoy." She leaned into his chest a bit more. She loved his arms wrapped around her.

"I knew I didn't want to buy anything and rent in Alaska can be stupid expensive so, one day, while reading the local freebie paper I saw Clara's classified ad with a room for rent. I instantly adored her. She was like a mom and a grandmother rolled into one. Always fussing at me. Trying to fix me up with her son — not in this life — and was planning on adopting me into her clan. That was supposed to happen next month actually." She smiled at the thought.

"She also cheated at cribbage, but I never could catch her. I think I might owe her just under ten thousand dollars. She was very special to me."

Kane wiped a stray tear away and kissed her cheek again.

"When I called Tuesday, Douglas told me she had the flu. I never thought I'd get a call telling me she died of a massive stroke." She paused for another moment.

"You know, he called me from a bar, he was half lit." She shook her head in disbelief.

"He wanted to make sure I'd stay on as his tenant with a small rent increase, of course, and did I have a key to the house? Her memorial will be the week after next." She looked up into his eyes and she so wanted to ask if he'd come.

How did he know?

"Becca would you like me to come and spend a few weeks with you in Sitka? Because I would be happy to." He kissed her lips.

She turned and wrapped her arms around him.

"Yes please. And can I still come stay with you in Bellingham, for a little while at least?"

That got a much stronger reaction.

He gave her a very passionate kiss. One that started her heart again.

He then put his lips to her ear. "My sweet woman, I want you to live with me and not for any little while."

The oven beeped and sort of messed up that special moment and they couldn't help but laugh.

*Nice tension reliever as well.*

Up again and loving her man more than ever, she got the baking sheet out and put eight strips of bacon on it before popping it in the oven for fifteen minutes.

She then got the ingredients out to whip up a batch of pancakes for both her guys.

She would still miss Clara but talking about it made her grief tolerable.

"Thank you for letting me ramble on. It helped." Her smile reached her eyes that time.

He got up and pulled her away from her task. Taking her face in his hands.

"Let's get one thing straight, you don't ramble, and I love that you were so candid about your life and your feelings. I hope you continue to talk to me all day long. I would love to listen." He finished with another kiss that made her a tad weak in the knees.

James' entrance brought them both back to reality.

"Good morning." And he ducked in the bathroom.

Becca poured him a cup of coffee when he entered the kitchen and pulled the now done bacon out of the oven and placed the crispy strips on the waiting paper towel.

She asked if either wanted eggs with their pancakes and bacon. Almost in unison they both said yes.

Back to the fridge she brought out the eggs and put jam, butter and syrup on the table along with hot sauce and ketchup.

"So, Jake is beyond pissed at his brother and me since I've screwed up the barbeque today. I told him to bring Justin and a few buddies and go water skiing. That way, the mountain of food you bought won't go to waste. But you have to save me a couple burgers if you wouldn't mind." He winked at his sister.

She loved how he didn't even ask if she minded the extra mouths, she didn't but still—

"Becs, you look pale. What's going on? You sick?" He was up getting another cup of coffee.

"I'm fine. Now, would you set the table so I can get breakfast finished." And with that turned back to whisking the eggs into a frothy mixture and getting the griddle up to temp.

Again, small kitchen.

"So, Curt... what's up with my sister this morning?" He pulled three plates down and put them by the griddle for her and grabbed silverware and napkins before taking his seat at the table.

'Damn he's nosy.' She shook her head and concentrated on cooking.

With the griddle nice and hot she spooned the pancake batter onto it and tried to keep them the same size.

HA! Always good in theory.

She heard Kane tell her brother about Clara with no other details.

At the same time, she was pouring the eggs into the now hot pan on the stove to get their scramble on.

Another weird familiar moment. Yep.

Freaky Fucking Sunday

"I'm so sorry Becs. That sucks out loud."

Sometimes he was as emotional as a wet hen.

But she knew he cared.

Pancakes flipped and stacked on a plate, she spooned four more pancakes on the griddle.

Eggs done and second batch of flapjacks almost ready. She dished up two rather large plates of food and deposited one in front of each man.

She had a few eggs on her plate since she wasn't hungry anyway and both her brother and Kane took one of their four slices of bacon off their plates and gave them to her.

She shook her head and smiled.

*Said it before… it's a bitch when you have two overbearing food monitors.*

Still, they did it out of love.

'Jackasses.'

She added hot sauce and a small bit of ketchup to her eggs which made Kane wince, but he didn't say a word once she was eating.

She was surprised to see him drown his pancakes in syrup.

Go figure.

He carried no extra weight and was quite fit.

He didn't have six pack abs, but he was firm all the same.

And had the most glorious ass. That thought was stirring her up a tad.

He squeezed her hand to bring her out of her head. He also nodded at her food directing her to finish.

She was blushing at him and took another bite. He had a questioning eyebrow up.

Her brother was oblivious to their exchange and took the last bite of his jam covered pancakes and asked for seconds, of course he did.

*Really, he should weigh so much more.*

She made him three additional cakes and that killed off the batter but mentioned to Kane that she'd be happy to make more if he wanted seconds.

He told her, 'No thank you,' he was quite satisfied.

But did ask her to come and finish her breakfast. He even said please.

Kane got up and started the dishwater and when Becca said she'd do that, he told her that he'd be cleaning up the kitchen that morning. No arguments.

How very sweet.

James caught that one. "Becs, looks like you have a real keeper with this one."

"I think so too." She had a huge smile on her face.

He gave her a quick peck on the cheek and thanked her for breakfast.

She cleared the dishes, handed them to Kane at the sink and put everything back in the fridge.

She also wiped down the griddle and got it stored once it cooled.

With James back at the bunkhouse getting fresh clothes for the day, Becca took a minute to caress Kane's very beautiful backside while his hands were in the hot dishwater.

"Becca, you'd better stop before your brother finds us in a very compromising position."

She reached around and ever so gently stroked the front of his groin feeling his somewhat hard penis.

"Damn you woman!"

She stopped and walked towards the bedroom.

The backdoor opened and James asked if anyone needed the bathroom for the next fifteen to twenty minutes. She told him it was all his.

She knew her brother very well. And he'd be a good half hour.

She winked at Kane who had his hands out the water and all over her seconds after he shut the bedroom door.

So very exhilarating with someone else in the cabin. A bit naughty.

Her thoughts about Kane during breakfast had her ready for his now fully erect penis and she was happy to feel him inside her again.

Biting her lip and his kept her from screaming out as she climaxed.

He bit down on her breast with his own release.

Her breathing was a tad erratic, but she managed a thank you.

"No sweetheart. Thank you. Damn you surprise me at every turn."

He slowly pulled out and she moaned, sorry to feel him go.

His tongue played with her ear, and she could feel herself getting wet again.

Damn, he's so very good.

"More baby."

She shook her head, but he didn't stop.

He was a force and climaxed through her aftershocks.

When James came out, showered and dressed, Kane was back finishing the dishes. Becca, who was still recovering, was making the bed with clean sheets.

"Okay you two, I'm off. See you tonight." Becca came out in her robe saying it was her turn for a shower gave her big brother a kiss goodbye and told him to give her great-nieces and great-nephew a hug from her. And to tell Mark he could 'kiss her ass'.

He just nodded and smiled at her. He also knew she wasn't kidding. Becca made an Olympic sport out of grudge holding. Something James knew all about… first hand.

She dashed into the bath and got into the shower before he asked any questions. She was sure he knew they had just had sex.

The shower felt nice on her skin. Not as nice as Kane's lips but nothing had or would ever top that.

She screamed when he suddenly pulled the curtain open.

"Jesus, Kane, you scared the shit out of me."

"This shower is beyond small. I wanted to join you." Her heart rate picked back up for another reason. That sounded so wonderful.

She shook her head. "Limited space so this is all we got. As a kid we bathed in the lake." With that, she closed the curtain and finished rinsing off.

He was still there to hand her a towel.

"Wait until I get you home. You're going to love the walk-in shower and the jetted tub at my house." He wrapped her up in the towel.

OKAY!

That seemed really scary familiar. Another Déjà vu.

'AGAIN! Fucking weird.'

He then ushered her out of the bathroom and shut the door.

'Oh, he needed it for another reason.'

She laughed and headed to pick out some clothes.

Shorts and a tank top would do.

Weatherman said it would be in the low nineties on this beautiful August day.

Of course, all her lotions and things were still in the bathroom, so she went ahead and got dressed waiting for her turn to go back in.

Being alone at the cabin had one major advantage... easy access to everything, no waiting.

When Kane emerged, he suggested she wait a few minutes but handed her a bottle of lotion, deodorant and her perfume bottle.

Very thoughtful and a bit clairvoyant.

Once fully scented and feeling much more put together, she went and sat next to him on the couch.

"So, how many siblings do you have? Are your parents alive? What's your house like? And while you're at it, what's your middle name."

There, she smiled, now it was his turn to illuminate her with some basic information.

He was wearing her favorite glacier melting smile.

"I have a sister and a brother. Sara is forty, lives in San Diego, she's a marine biologist and has lived with her life partner, Erika, for just under seventeen years now. They have two very spoiled cats. Both calicos named Rosemary and Thyme. Peter is forty-nine and he and his wife, Naomi, live in Tulsa with their two kids. Samuel and Ruth and before you ask, yes, they are very religious. He is in fact a pastor, and his wife teaches kindergarten, and no, we are not close. Both my folks are alive and kicking in Phoenix were my dad retired six years ago. And my middle name is in fact James." He gave her a quick kiss and headed into the kitchen.

He returned with waters for each of them.

He continued his history once he retook her hand.

"My house in Bellingham was a major fixer upper when I bought it seven years ago. I sort of gutted the whole thing. From the outside it looks like a classic Tudor-style home but once inside it takes on a whole new feeling."

She could tell he was proud of his home.

"The top floor is the master bedroom, master bath and my office. The main floor is the kitchen, sitting room, TV room and two guest rooms, each has their own bath. The basement is gym, laundry and storage. The property is just under ten acres in total with a three-car garage and an old barn I just can't bring myself to tear down."

He took a long drink of water looking at her reaction.

She really didn't have one.

"It sounds beautiful — and big — you're one guy... did you build it for a woman in your life at the time?" She was a bit perceptive as well.

"Yes and no. At the time I purchased it, I was in a fairly serious relationship, and she wanted to run a B & B. So, I designed the four-thousand-five-hundred-square-foot home with that in mind on the ground floor only, the upstairs was all about what I wanted. We weren't together by the time I got finished."

He was caressing the knuckles on her hand.

"Before you ask, I've never been married, and I've only come close once and I thank the stars for keeping that from happening." He leaned over and gave her a very tender kiss.

"Where did you and Carl meet?" She was on a roll with questions.

"Washington State University, we were in the same dorm as freshmen. He hit on me one night when he'd had way too much to drink, and I put him to the floor with one punch. We've been the best of friends ever since." He laughed at that memory.

She again shocked him.

"You're a fucking cougar. Get out!" She couldn't contain her laughter since his look was priceless.

"Very funny Becca. So, I'm guessing you went to the University of Idaho since the schools are like what, eight miles apart? You know they haven't really been rivals in a decade or two now." He smirked at her.

She leaned in and gave him a kiss, "Okay, you can stay then."

He kissed her back with a bit more force.

"Why thank you." And his grin made her whole body, flush.

"I'm going to go take a shower and after I'd like to chat about an outing for tomorrow." She nodded.

He showered quickly and was now in the bedroom putting on a pair of shorts and nothing else.

'Damn he is one handsome man.' She loved looking at him, but she also liked spending time with him, just talking or sitting quietly and holding hands.

"When are your nephew and friends invading us? Didn't you say something about three p.m. for the barbeque?" He was just coming back into the living room.

"He texted a few minutes ago, should be here around noon and yes that was the plan but with James at the park, we can do it a bit later or even a bit earlier."

Then she asked about the mysterious outing he had planned for the next day.

His phone interrupted them.

It was Carl checking in and letting Kane know that the boat was safely loaded, and he and Warren would be heading back home after they had some breakfast, and they'd see him in a week.

He mentioned he might be going to Alaska for a few weeks and would he mind holding down the fort.

Apparently, he didn't since Kane told him he was a good man and hung up.

"Outing?" She was more than inquisitive now.

"I would like to take you shopping. And I want you to just say yes without over thinking and without asking me a dozen questions."

He had a sheepish grin.

"Can I ask one question at least?" She knew something was up.

"One and that's it." Stern but sexy

"Why?" Then she sat back and waited.

"Because I want too. Now, let's go enjoy the day. How about a swim?" He was back wearing her smile.

That threw her off her game. He never wanted to swim. And that glacier melting smile of his was throwing her off completely.

She nodded since she knew he wasn't going to reveal anything else.

'That's frustrating.'

*And if you're wondering... yes, another déjà vu moment.*

They didn't change into suits but did go down to sit on the dock and enjoy the fully awake morning sun.

The lake was getting busy, and the jet-skis started to make their appearances.

*Nope, still not a fan.*

But Becca did noticed Kane was looking a bit envious of the loud ass machines.

Without really thinking, she told him that he could rent one down at Bottle Bay Marina if he wanted.

They were stupid expensive, but it was the closest location.

She kind of wished she knew her neighbors better and then maybe she could have just borrowed one.

But then again, who knew she'd meet someone. That was a huge shocker, still was a bit.

"Would you like to ride one of your own or would you ride with me?" He winked at her. Apparently, he liked the idea.

"Mr Kane, I believe you've rode me enough, perhaps you should go solo on this one." She had her own sheepish grin on her face.

"Ms Sims, I am nowhere close to being done, riding you." His look was quite sensual.

DAMN... where the hell, did he come from?
*Can we clone him? Please.*

She felt her whole body, shudder at that statement.

He took ownership of her lips and all within. When he pulled away, he whispered, "Looks like jet-skiing will have to wait until later." And with that he cupped her ass as he walked her up to the cabin.

She was beyond ready when they made it into the bedroom. Her body craved his, almost to the point of scaring her.

'What if he leaves?' She knew her world would crumple into desolation.

'Becs stop thinking negative thoughts.' She was still good at scolding herself.

Kane's phone started ringing off the hook, so to speak.

Coitus Interruptus! Well, that sucks!

He answered with a bit of harshness to his tone. "Hello. Okay. No! Yes, that would be fine. Hold on please." Then he turned to Becca. "How do I explain my exact location?" She reached for his phone, and he handed it over.

She told the faceless voice on the other end how to find her cabin and hung up.

She handed Kane back his phone and waited.

He was flush with anger and the waning passion coursing through his veins, so it took a few minutes for him to settle down.

"They are sending the launch for me. Apparently 'Daddy's Girl' has a few issues and I've been summoned." His tone was quite acidic.

Becca reminded him that it was his reputation on the line and that a happy customer will result in great reviews for future business.

"You're amazing and you're right. I just don't know how long I'll be so may I please have a rain check regarding this unforeseen interruption?" He was almost wearing her favorite smile. She could see he was still a bit miffed.

Becca nodded and gave him a nice kiss.

The launch was already approaching… 'Damn, that was fast.'

While Kane threw on a polo shirt and changed out of flip-flops into deck shoes… Becca waved at the advancing boat to let them know they had the right place.

He gave her another nice kiss before heading to the dock and boarding his transport.

She waved as he and his ride headed back towards Hope.

Feeling a bit… tense herself… Becca decided a nice cool swim was in order.

*A nice LONG swim if you must know.*

The lake felt wonderful and cooled every fiber of her body, thank goodness for small favors.

She heard her phone and decided nothing at that moment needed her attention.

She was playing with her lake and having a ball.

She thought she heard her phone again but wasn't sure.

Proud of herself for doing six laps down to the bunkhouse and back she climbed out onto the dock and waited for the sun to warm her now chilled body.

Her phone rang again. JEEZ!

'Who the hell would be burning up her phone on a Sunday?'

Wrapped in her towel she climbed the stairs up to the cabin and looked at the five missed calls… all from Kane.

She took her phone and a bottle of water and headed back to the dock.

He had left her three messages.

The first was short:

*Don't swim until Jake is there, please.*

The second:

*Becca, where are you? Get out of the lake and answer.*

The third and final one:

*I am getting a tad concerned that you're still not answering. This is why I don't like you to swim without supervision. CALL ME!*

He didn't leave a message after the fourth or fifth call, so she knew he was beside himself. 'Talk about over thinking.'

With a huge sigh and knowing he was going to be upset with her, she hit redial.

She got his voicemail. "Hi, all good here. See you when you get back and I'm sorry if I worried you." She tried to sound as upbeat as she could.

How in the hell was she going to get him over the swimming phobia? Could she?

Supervision was a bit over the top as well since she'd been swimming in her lake for over fifty years. Still, his concern was kind of endearing.

Her eyes were closed, and she was enjoying the warmth of the day when she heard the boat.

Her heart jumped into her throat, 'Would he still be miffed?'

When she opened her eyes and saw Jake, she felt a little relieved and a little sad. She missed Kane. Mad or not.

She waved, stood and grabbed the rope he threw.

Jake owned a Master Craft ProStar, a perfect boat on the lake. Great for skiing and wakeboarding. He was very proud of it and kept it in immaculate condition which always surprised her since she knew how he kept his room growing up. She used to call him 'pig pen' and that's what he named the boat.

*Freud would have a field day with her family.*

He brought Justin, his other buddy Brian and two young women wearing very 'itsy bitsy' bikinis.

Not much left to the imagination with those suits. She now knew both women waxed.

She shook her head... 'Oh to be young.'

She wondered which one belonged with her nephew.

Jake was thirty-five and buff in his five-foot-ten frame. He had bleached blond hair and icy blue eyes. Very attractive. Looked a lot like his dad without the excess poundage.

He put the bumpers down so his boat would be protected from the dock and got off giving his aunt a nice hug. Being 'anal' must be a trait on the male side of her family. The dock had built in bumpers already.

"Hey Aunt Becs, this is Sam and Tiffany." Both women waved and Becca said hello to each of them.

He asked where Curtis was, and she let him know that he was working on an issue on the yacht he built.

"Seen that huge ass boat yesterday. Impressive."

Justin and Brian started to unload their towels and cooler onto the dock before each man helped the ladies out of the boat and onto the dock.

Becca then got a huge hug from Brian, who she hadn't seen since last summer and, of course, Justin took his turn.

Brian was a year younger than Jake, two inches shorter and weighed about fifty pounds more. He looked up to her nephew like a big brother and would follow him everywhere.

He also, for some weird reason, had always had a crush on Becca.

Being old enough to be his mom she thought that had a wee bit of an ick factor. But was flattered all the same.

Truth was, as stated earlier, she felt like a cougar having Kane in her life. She'd never go with anyone in their thirties.

When Brian made puppy dog eyes at Becca, Jake threw him in the lake.

"She's taken and you're sick. Fucking A!" He smiled and winked at his aunt.

That was her cue to head back into the cabin and organize the barbeque and get back into her shorts and tank top.

One of the Bobbsey twins knocked asking to use the powder room.

*The Bobbsey Twins were first introduced in a book series by Harper Lee Hope and Howard R Garis that published in 1904. Now it means two people who look similar and act alike. In case you hadn't heard the phrase and were wondering.*

Becca had to laugh and showed her where it was.

She also told her on the way out that she didn't need to knock next time.

Youth is totally wasted on the young.

Changed and with pen and pad in hand she headed back to the dock to get a burger and dog count for the barbeque.

She wasn't surprised when the JJs asked for two of each. They could eat. Brian sheepishly asked for one of each, Becca wrote down two, just in case.

The ladies asked for a burger each but no bun… of course they did.

She added her brother's request for two burgers and put down two for Kane in the hopes he'd be back in time.

Once inside she organized all the food on the table to see what she had.

Happy with four family-sized bags of chips, buns, cheese, relish, condiments, baked beans and chili plus all the veggies for the burgers… she got busy cutting up some fresh fruit to add to the mix. She'd wait on getting the burger toppings ready until they were about to eat.

With so much food she decided that she didn't need to worry about making desert.

Happy that everything was virtually prepped, Becca decided to sit on the upper deck and watch the young one's ski, for a while. She tended to burn so she was mindful not to get too much sun.

Jake was a natural on a wakeboard… and Justin was damn near as good but poor Brian, he just didn't have the knack and fell a half dozen times before he gave up and swam to shore.

He was sitting by himself on the dock as the boys tried to get Bobbsey twin two up on skis but were having a difficult time.

She could totally relate to them since she never could get the hang of skiing either and wakeboarding wasn't a thing when she was growing up on the water.

This would be the main reason she was such a good swimmer.

Becca began to feel bad for Brian and decided to go and have a chat.

"What's going on with you these days?" She smiled and sat down next to him.

He shrugged.

Being somewhat perceptive, she asked, "Which one do you like?" She winked at him.

He blushed.

How cute.

"Samantha but she likes Jake and would never go for me." He looked so downtrodden.

She asked which one was Sam and found out she was, indeed, Bobbsey twin number one.

"So, Tiffany is into Justin?" And when he shook his head... her only thought was, 'That nut didn't fall too far from the tree.'

"Brian, have you asked her out or told her how you feel? You might be surprised." She wasn't totally convinced of this statement but then again, Kane was a complete shock to her.

Once in a while you have to root for the underdog.

"Do you really think that or are you just being nice?" He had a dubious look on his face.

Busted!

She told him a bit of both but that doesn't make her advice bad.

*Like stated, Kane was a complete and wondrous shock to her. So, here's to everyone finding that special someone.*

She then asked which girl did Jake like and found out it was Bobbsey twin two leaving Sam out in the cold.

She understood what Brian was going through since she was like him growing up. Never having a boyfriend or being asked out on dates in high school.

"Look sweetie, you have to make your own choices in this life and find your happiness. You're a great guy with a lot to offer. You really do deserve to find someone to love. You might get hurt a few times but with any adventure, there is risk." She patted his hand and stood to go start prepping the burgers.

To her surprise Brian wrapped his arms around her in a big bear hug. She was hugging him back when she saw the launch coming back with her own love.

He released her when he heard the boat. Most likely thinking it was Jake and he'd be thrown back into the water for hugging her.

Kane stepped off and pushed the launch back off the dock.

He was eyeing Brian with a bit of venom, so Becca introduced him to Jake's young friend.

Kane shook his hand, but his expression was still evasive.

Brian took that as a good time to throw himself in the lake.

Kane walked over and gave her a kiss without much feeling.

"Am I getting too old for you... you trying for twenty years younger now? I wonder how he'll compare as a lover?" His vile questions hit her harder than a slap in the face and he shouldn't have been standing so close to the dock's edge.

She shoved him backwards and he was quite surprised. And now, quite wet.

She waited for Curt to resurface, coughing up some of the lake he managed to swallow and then unleashed on him for being the biggest jackass that walked the planet.

"Fuck you and the horse you rode in. I've watched that boy grow up, you are one sick motherfucker! You're also no longer welcome here." She was seeing red, and the altercation was witnessed by her nephew who was just bringing his boat back to the dock.

She headed back up the stairs without looking back and locked every door in the cabin but not before leaving his bag of clothes on the top deck. He's lucky they didn't end up in the lake.

Becca was so angry she couldn't contain her tears and that made her even madder. She took the key to the back door and hiked up to the high meadow.

A little distance was needed, and it was the best place to be alone with her murderous thoughts.

Thirty minutes or so later she had finally calmed down so even the tears stopped and she was mentally talking to her grandfather.

She wasn't surprised to see Jake arrive.

"Hey Aunt Becs, you, okay? Can I sit?" She nodded.

He took her hand.

"He feels like a total jerk, and we all gave him a good talking to, but he needs to see you. Becca, he loves you. And besides, I'm starving, and you have the cabin locked up." He squeezed her hand and smiled at her.

Still her favorite.

"Here's the key to the back door. Go start the burgers and dogs. And you can send the fucking asshole up here." She was feeling more hurt than angry now that she had had time to think.

"Way to keep a positive spin on the situation." He got an evil look from his aunt and kissed her on the cheek and headed back to the cabin.

It was maybe ten or so minutes later when she heard him call her. He didn't know where the high meadow was and got himself a bit lost.

'Jackass!'

She found him in less than a minute.

When he approached like he was going to hug her, she backed away from him with her arms folded around herself.

"Say what you came to say and go." She was hurt and mad at herself for letting someone break down her walls. She would rather spend the rest of her life alone than endure the pain she felt at that moment.

*NOT that she didn't have enough reasons to feel the way she was feeling.*

*Still, little drama queen in us all.*

He took a deep breath. "I was so jealous seeing you hugging that young man. And mad that I had to leave earlier and then I couldn't get a hold of you. And I didn't get your message until I was on the way back to the cabin. And frustrated with the new owner of the yacht. Becca, I just lashed out so you'd feel as bad as me, but I had no idea I would get that reaction and I'm so sorry. Please forgive me for being a stupid fucking idiot."

She could tell he was being sincere. He had very expressive eyes and they showed her the sadness he felt.

Continuing since she wasn't responding he said, "Your nephew and his friends were very passionate when it came to scolding me and Justin went so far as to threaten me. And they were right to do so, my behavior was inexcusable. I know you are not that kind of woman, and I will spend the rest of my life making it up to you, if you'll let me. Please let me." He opened up his arms.

She walked into his arms, and he folded them around her. "Oh Becca, I will never hurt you like that again... you have my word." With that she put her arms around him.

He asked if he could kiss her, and she gave him a firm 'no' but smiled and he knew she was forgiving him.

He didn't ask a second time, he just took possession of her lips and tongue and laid her down on the soft moss in the meadow.

He pulled off her shorts and worked his magic. "Sweetheart, I want you here and now!" And with that he slid deep inside her.

She'd never even thought of having sex outside, but she and her body were very happy they did.

'Wow, make-up sex is... HOT!'

"That was unexpected." She had a smirk on her face.

He kissed her hair. "Yes, it was Beautiful, thank you for forgiving me."

She nodded and jumped scaring them both when something crawled on her leg.

That gave her the willies and she was shaking out her shorts before she put them on. Kane was brushing moss off of her back, spending a bit too much time on her bare butt.

She turned and gave him a quick kiss and told him she'd wait until they were in a bed for any further attention to her ass.

"That's a date." And he smacked her pretty good before she could pull on her shorts.

Again, HOT!

They walked down the hill and back towards the cabin hand in hand.

When Jake saw them, he smiled.

"Glad you two came to your senses. You look great as a couple. But you hurt my aunt again, Curt, they won't find the body." He chuckled at both their expressions.

Becca decided to ignore the threat but did notice that the hamburgers were almost done, and the hotdogs were good and charred.

She and Kane went and cut up the onions, tomatoes, pickles and lettuce as toppers and she also put out slices of three different kinds of cheese.

Justin had put the chili on the stove as well as baked beans and must have opened all the chips... good boy.

She also retrieved the fruit salad she'd made earlier and added it to the array of choices. Becca then got all the condiments out along with paper plates, napkins, silverware and put everything in a buffet setup so everyone could help themselves.

Number one rule of the cabin: no one should ever leave hungry.

It was just after four when Jake called everyone to eat, and Becca heard a truck on the hill.

"Looks like your dad made it back in time for food." She smiled since he never seemed to miss a meal.

That also made her realize that she'd not eaten since breakfast. Explained the mild headache she had been feeling for the past couple hours.

The disturbing afternoon didn't really help with that either.

It seemed like such a long time ago when she and Kane were talking about the death of her dear landlady, and it was actually just a few hours earlier. She smiled thinking she'd been on a bit of a roller coaster herself this day, emotionally speaking at least.

James came in bearing gifts from the amusement park, an assortment of T-shirts, bumper stickers, key rings and candy. Sometimes he forgot his kids ... weren't kids any more.

He also handed Becca a note from Mark.

*Dear Aunt, Bec's,*

*I totally suck as a nephew and I'm so sorry I've not come to visit with you this summer. The kids and I would love to come out Wednesday if you are agreeable. And 'no' Amy will not be coming.*

*My situation is unique to say the least, but I shouldn't deprive my kids of knowing my favorite aunt. Love, Mark*

Jake grabbed the note.

"Hey, you little shit, give it back!" But he knew she was teasing.

"Man, my brother can be a suck up. Don't buy it Aunt Becs, he's just trying to get back into your will." He smiled and took the biggest bite out of his burger she'd ever seen.

A little gross actually.

"Jake, I think your brother just wants to do the right thing." Scolded by his father. Jake just rolled his eyes and gave her a wink.

Yep, still her favorite.

She went and got her phone and texted Mark that Wednesday would be wonderful. She even added two hearts.

"Shit!" And looked at Kane.

He was smiling at her and nodded.

It dawned on her at that precise moment that she had pushed him in the lake with his phone in his pocket.

She looked a bit mortified and told him she was sorry.

"No, you're not." He had a wicked smile.

Truth was… he brought it upon himself, so she really wasn't.

She shrugged.

"Well, we'll just have to add that to the shopping list for tomorrow." And with that she got her own plate started.

"Did I miss a page or two… what are you apologizing for?" James looked at his sister very confused.

Jake being ever helpful… or not.

"Curt there pissed off Aunt Bec's, so she pushed him in the lake and pretty much trashed his phone. But he really deserved it and now they've had make-up sex so all's good."

"Thank you for that very concise and matter of fact *Reader's Digest* version of the event, nephew." She wasn't smiling at him.

Her brother, who wasn't fond of conflict, which would explain his three marriages, told everyone to get their plates and eat on the dock.

That cleared out of the cabin, right quick.

Becca finished making her lettuce wrap burger and took some fruit salad.

Other than the Bobbsey twins, she had the least amount of food.

Kane it would seem liked burnt hotdogs and made three with everything.

That actually made her smile since those used to be her favorite item to eat as a kid. The blacker the better. Weird but true.

Just James, Kane and Becca remained in the cabin, and they all decided to eat in the living room.

James even gave them the couch and sat in the chair across.

They were well into their meals when James brought the silence to an end.

"You got off easy Curt. I think the last time I pissed my little sister off that bad, it took her seven years to forgive me." James looked almost jealous of that.

"Long time ago James and major water under the bridge. I think we've moved on nicely since then." She looked at her brother with a 'change the fucking subject before I kill you look'.

Kane being ever observant couldn't quite let that one go.

"What in the world did you do? I want to make sure I never make the same error. Mine was bad enough." After his tense afternoon he was more than a bit curious.

"Becs, I only brought it up since you're mad at Mark and I want you to forgive him. He loves that dingy broad and we all have to accept that." His look was more pleading.

She nodded. Staying mad at the nephews was harder since she only had two and she didn't have kids and never would.

*Of course, one could challenge that she only had one brother, but her situation was different then, he had abandoned her, right when she needed him the most. At least that's how it felt at the time.*

She lost some of her appetite but finished her fruit. Kane gave her a stern look and asked her to please eat more.

Tired of fighting with anyone she managed a couple more bites before throwing her plate away.

The JJs were back for seconds, or thirds and she wondered where in the hell they put all that food. They both thanked her for the grub, and she told them to thank Kane, he bought everything.

They both had their mouths full when they thanked him.

'AGAIN... GROSS.' Maybe they were adolescents after all.

He just smiled and nodded.

The universal guy gesture for 'you're welcome'.

Once her brother got his second plate and Kane said he was quite stuffed, she got to work putting everything away and organizing the refrigerator while she was at it.

She was also eavesdropping on James and Kane's conversation since it pertained to her. She knew she wasn't going to be able to stop James from retelling that horrid tale, so she tried to keep herself busy.

"About nineteen years ago now, the boys were both in school, Jake was being a hellion, I was in the process of moving my construction company to Montana and my third marriage was coming to an end, so I was beyond preoccupied. I got a letter from Bec's, and she was in bad shape about her own marriage, and I didn't get the gist so instead of being a good big brother and reaching out to her, I emailed her telling her to get a divorce if she wasn't happy. And that was the last time I heard from her for seven years." He was actually tearing up.

Becca came in and handed him a tissue. "James, stop please."

"Becca, I didn't know. I didn't understand how bad you were hurt." He was up and had her in a hug and they were both crying.

"Would you have ever told me if I hadn't found the letter you wrote to Mom?"

She shook her head.

He let her go and went and blew his nose and composed himself.

"You missed Mark's wedding because of me. That's why Amy doesn't like you." It was his way of making the wrong right.

*Mark had sworn his dad to secrecy to protect his wife and spare hurting his aunt's feelings.*

She nodded.

Trying to lighten the mood. "I sent them a thousand bucks. Tell her to get the fuck over it."

James laughed and kissed his sister's cheek. "I love you, sis."

"Now I think, I'll go to take a dip in that freezing ass lake of ours. Thanks for dinner Curt." And off he went leaving Kane staring at Becca.

"Becca, will you ever tell me the rest of that saga? Did your ex physically hurt you? Because I would like to hunt him down and kill him right about now."

She shook her head to the whole statement and went to finish up in the kitchen.

He followed her and took her into his embrace. She loved his hugs and melted into his arms.

Their moment was interrupted by Bobbsey twin two needing the bathroom.

They both chuckled at her blush.

Again, not much material in that bikini of hers.

"Well, that doesn't leave a lot to the imagination," Kane was shaking his head.

She brought his lips to hers and, of course, he took it much further.

A small cough got them to end a rather intimate kiss and they both looked over at a very embarrassed Brian.

"Tiffany's in there so you'll have to wait your turn." And with that she finished tiding up the kitchen.

Kane went out on the porch to fetch his bag, giving her a rather loud smack on the ass as he passed her and went into the bedroom closing the door.

He came out a minute later in his swim trunks.

"Get on your suit woman, we're going swimming in your lake." He had on her favorite smile.

Becca actually clapped her hands and went and got her suit off the railing.

She was beyond thrilled.

The sun was on its downward trajectory, but it was still warm enough to take a dip. And there were a few hours left before it actually set.

Her brother was on the dock, wet. He must have jumped in and gotten right back out. Funny, she usually heard him scream.

'Wimp.'

Jake and Justin were packing up the skis and wakeboard along with towels and their cooler.

"You off for town already? It was nice meeting you girls and don't take any shit from these yahoo's." She then gave her nephew a nice hug and then Justin.

"We'll leave as soon as Brian finishes stinking up the cabin." He had his dad's smile.

She shook her head and was just a bit surprised when Kane threw her in the lake.

When she came up for air the whole dock was laughing. She beckoned him to join her, and he did.

When he reached her, she put her arms around his neck and gave him a very loving kiss.

"Hey, you two, not in front of the children." James was chuckling.

Brian was just coming down and Jake made some sarcastic statement about keeping them all waiting and got a stern look from his dad.

Brian thanked Becca for having him and got on the boat looking a bit gloomy. She waved and told him she'd see him next summer.

Jake gave his dad a big hug and yelled, "Love you," to his aunt and with that... the youngsters were off.

She still was wrapped in Kane's arms when James headed inside.

Once they were alone in her lake, she gave him a very passionate kiss.

He moaned her name and she let go and disappeared under the water.

She came up slowly behind him caressing his ass and quickly removed his swim trucks.

She then disappeared again but this time she was a good twenty feet away.

"Damn you Becca. Get back here."

She shook her head.

"How are those lower extremities working now?" She winked and continued swimming away as he started to gain ground.

'Shit, he's a really good swimmer, didn't plan on that one.'

She still managed to beat him to the ladder and made it on the dock before he emerged.

She could tell he wasn't totally aroused but his look was very primal.

She graciously handed him back his trucks which he dropped and wrapped a towel around his waist all the while grabbing her and putting his lips on hers.

"Bedroom. Now." It was his lustful growl. Which was a huge turn on.

She wanted to protest since James was currently in the living room, more than likely having a beer and watching some sports channel but she wanted him as much as he wanted her.

They went up the back way and she was surprised it was open. Jake must have unlocked all the doors after getting the key from her earlier.

Becca then went and quietly shut the bedroom door. When she turned, he was naked. Well, he only had a towel on to start with, then motioned for her to get out of her suit.

She did and found herself flat on her back with him taking ownership of her lips and tongue. His fingers had her nipples hard in seconds.

"Roll over baby, I'm taking you from behind."

She instantly tensed at a very unhappy memory from her past and started to shake her head.

Kane took her face in his hands and whispered ever so softly, "I'm not him. Have some faith in me, please."

He rolled her over and caressed her ass and she started to feel better and incredibly aroused by his touch.

His fingers moved in and out of her and all her tension left her body, replaced by her want for this man.

When he entered her, it felt amazing and as he started thrusting, her body matched his cadence until they both exploded in dual orgasms.

He wrapped her into his arms and nuzzled her neck. "Thank you for trusting me sweetheart." She smiled and nodded and held tight onto his arms.

Another ugly memory replaced with a very pleasant one.

When Becca woke the room was dark and she was alone.

She heard voices in the outer room and debated whether to just stay in the cozy bed or go see what her men folk were doing.

She stretched, dressed and headed into the living room after snagging a water and was not surprised to see both eating leftovers and watching a baseball game, yep Mariners.

"Sis, you need to exercise more, sex shouldn't knock you on your ass like that." She slugged him as hard as she could in his shoulder.

He grinned and rubbed his shoulder. Mouthing a silent ouch.

She went and gave Kane a kiss and sat on the floor by his legs. He stroked her hair and asked her to please eat something.

She was going to say 'no' but since she still had a bit of a headache, decided a snack might be a good idea.

Becca came back with apple slices and a tablespoon of peanut butter and sat back down on the floor again putting her head against his leg.

Kane didn't give her any grief on her food choice.

Instead, he thanked her for eating.

She wondered if James warned him about picking his battles or maybe he decided on his own to lighten up a bit.

Either way it made her smile.

They watched the game until it came to its conclusion, Seattle lost six-two.

Neither man was very happy with that outcome.

Kane was stroking her hair. Becca finished her apple slices, loving his touch.

James got up and took his plate and put it in the sink. "Okay you two, I'm bushed so I'm heading down to the bunkhouse. Feel free to make as much noise as you wish." He winked at his sister and bent down and gave her a peck on the cheek.

"Sleep well James, see you in the morning for breakfast." He nodded as he took his leave.

She looked at Kane who had a strange look on his face.

"What?"

She knew it was an 'I have questions but I'm nervous to ask' look.

"Could we just go to bed so I can hold you all night long?"

She nodded and turned off the TV, the side lamp and locked the cabin's front door but left the back door unlocked in case James needed the facilities.

After they both put their plates in the sink, Kane took her hand and led her into the bedroom.

He undressed her first and escorted her under the covers. He undressed with the light on so she could watch and then turned them off and climbed in beside her.

Best show in town.

Beat the hell out of the Mariners.

He started to caress her breasts and she was feeling it all the way down her body.

He leaned in and started to kiss the nape of her neck and she was responding to his very sensual touch.

"Mmmm... I thought you just wanted to hold me?" Her breathing was erratic, she was alive with desire for this man.

His fingers found her wet and ready. "Not before I give you an orgasm or two."

She reached for his penis, and he stopped her. "This is for you and only you, my girl." And continued to finger fuck her into her first release. He moved down with this tongue and was working on her second.

"Please Kane… you… I want to feel you."

Not able to refuse her he was her final release and followed quickly after.

'Holy Crap.'

She was beyond spent and laid in his arms falling asleep.

"Becca, your brother told me the whole story from earlier today and I wanted you to know. We never have to discuss it, or we can if you want. And I love you."

Her breathing told him she was fast asleep. He joined her.

# MONDAY

Becca was up early, showered and had the fire going, fresh biscuits were already in the oven, coffee made and even her numbers tested fairly good on this wonderful Monday morning.

She was setting the table when Kane emerged from their bedroom giving her a nice good morning kiss.

He also gave her a disapproving look since she was dressed for the day and told her he wouldn't mind helping her out of that outfit if she was so inclined.

She asked for her own rain check and got a much more passionate request.

Damn him!

She didn't have to find her resolve when the back door opened, and James ducked into the bathroom after bidding them a good morning.

Kane shook his head and gave her his best pout and headed back into the bedroom to put on clothes.

Even his pout was sexy.

'FUCK!'

Now, with everyone awake she went ahead and started the sausage gravy. She not only put sausage in the gravy, she also made huge sausage patties to top each biscuit, it made for an even heartier breakfast.

She figured James would be taking off between eight and nine that morning at the latest for his very long drive home and she didn't want him to have to stop for food for several hours.

They really didn't get much of a visit, but it was great to see him all the same. She really would have to go and spend some time in Billings next year.

She was pulling the biscuits out of the oven when both Kane and James came in for coffee. She retrieved the fruit salad from the day before since it would add something fresh to an otherwise heavy meal. Becca had them come dish up their own plates, so she didn't overfeed them. Again.

She tended to make way too much food. Came from not cooking all that often. She snagged a yogurt out of the fridge and put it in a bowl with some of the fruit salad. Kane cut one of his two sausage patties in half and put it on the side of her bowl.

When she rolled her eyes, he gave her a very stern look, the one that wasn't at all sexy.

To appease him she picked up the breakfast meat and took a bite.

Again... way to familiar... 'Is this all in the daydream that I had less than a week ago? Wow.' She shook her head bringing her back to the here and now.

Yep. Freaking Fucking Monday!

Her brother had devoured his first plate and was heading back for seconds.

She smiled.

She got up for another cup of coffee, her third that morning but it tasted really good.

Her brother took a refill, but Kane didn't.

Again, the one cup of coffee still killed her... who only has one cup?

*Well... Kane apparently.*

"So coffee is supposed to increase the appetite. Seems to have the opposite effect on you." He was looking at her with a very questioning look.

She asked if that was why he only had one cup. Ignoring his statement.

He shook his head and told her that a few years back he lived on the stuff and got an ulcer so now he had to keep his intake in check.

A bit more information about his life. He knew way too much about hers.

She had heard his confession the night before and his final statement that still made her heart swell.

She had perfected the sleep breathing while married to the 'fucking bastard' she now just called 'the ex'.

He took her hand to bring her back to him, "Over thinking sweetheart? Please finish eating your breakfast."

She looked at her bowl and it was over half eaten. His plate was empty, and her brother was currently spreading butter and jam on his fourth or fifth biscuit.

"Where did you want to go shopping?" She was changing the subject.

She also remembered she owed him a new phone.

"We'll go into Spokane later this morning. So, you have time to eat." He knew what she was attempting to do.

"Well, Curt, I'm going to leave you to argue with my sister about eating this time around. I'm going to head down and pack. Be back in twenty to shower and get ready for my long drive." He picked his plate up and deposited in the sink.

He then gave Becs a nice kiss on the cheek with a thank you for another wonderful breakfast.

"For a woman who doesn't like to eat, you sure know how to cook." And left out the front door.

She rolled her eyes at her brother since he knew she spent most of her life overweight.

'Jackass.'

"Becca!" Kane was staring at her when she got back out of her head.

She wasn't there that long, get a grip.

"I think we are going to add eye rolling to the mix today as well as over thinking." His look was stern.

This put a more than confused look on her face.

"What mix? Or do I even want to know?" She stood to clear the table and he grabbed her hand.

"Finish first and I'll do the dishes."

She picked up the remaining sausage and put it back on his plate and took the last two bites of yogurt.

"I got the dishes." And with that she was up and at the sink.

When his hand hit her ass, it wasn't at all arousing, in fact it hurt.

He had her trapped at the sink. "I will in fact take you over my knee today if you so much as think the 'f' word, roll your eyes at me, get lost in your head or argue about anything I wish to buy you. Is that clear?"

She nodded.

He then turned her so his lips could take possession of hers.

When he let her up for air, both their breathing was a bit ragged. "You will also eat lunch and dinner without argument." He turned her back to the sink and gave her another smack on the ass.

The second one was much more stimulating.

'What the fuck?' She really couldn't help herself.

Thank goodness he was in the living room by then.

James was back just as she was finishing up in the kitchen.

While he headed in for his shower, she went in and made the bed and grabbed her meds, avoiding Kane for a few more minutes.

She wondered how pissed he was going to be when she bought him his new phone, she caused the death of his current one, it was only right.

"Over thinking so soon?" He was actually grinning at her. And advancing.

"No, I was not, so just stay right where you are." She realized her heart was beating a bit fast.

"I warned you Becca." He was smirking at her.

"Kane, stop. I was not over thinking. I was wondering if you'd let me buy you a new phone, that's all." She was backed into the corner.

He reached her and gave her a kiss and then told her 'No' she wasn't allowed to do that. And even though she did in fact kill his phone, it was his fault for provoking her in the first place.

He felt her whole body relax in his arms and told her that he wasn't going to spank her for thinking and to please not worry about it.

He just wanted her to be aware that certain proclivities she had, tended to get his hackles up so today she would have consequences if and when she did them.

"Today only?" She wanted to put down a few of her own rules since he was 'Quirky'.

He nodded.

"I don't think I should get admonished for thinking a word, but I will try not to say it out loud. Will that work for your 'Quirky' self?" She was nothing if not impertinent.

"Becca, do you really think being sassy is the right move today? But I will give you that, 'one point' with the caveat, that you need to think it a lot less."

She pushed him back so she could leave the room. "Fine."

His chuckling made her mad.

Maybe she needed to give him a few fucking rules to follow.

He passed her slapping her ass hard. "Thinking it."

"Ass!" She couldn't help but shake her head.

His smile could and would have impressed the Cheshire cat.

James was out of the bathroom freshly showered and dressed for the day.

"I hate to basically eat and run but I have to get on the road. Becca I'm sorry we didn't really have a chance to talk. I'll try to get north one of these days and please come stay with me next summer. I love you, sis." And with that he pulled her into a nice bear hug.

"Love you too James. Please text me so I know you got home safely, and I will come see you next summer." She also hated that they really didn't have any time together. But enjoyed the visit they did have.

He shook Kane's hand and told him to take good care of his sister.

Then, very unlike James, asked Becca to walk him to his truck.

When they made it up the hill he turned and confessed. "I told Curt the rest of the story and I don't want you to be mad at me. I did it because he needs to know how hurt you've been and how to take care of you. He loves you Becs. Don't push him away… let him in. Share your darkness with him so he understands. I don't think even I know the whole story, do I?" He had that brotherly look that told her how much he cared.

Her tears told him he was right. "I can't. He knows too much. So, do you."

Mary was the only one who knew all the sordid details and she took them to her grave.

His hugs reminded her of their dad's. Strong and loving. Jake gave the same kind of hug too. She wasn't mad at him… she loved him.

He kissed her cheek and wiped the tears away. "Okay. I'll try and let it go. Love you, Becs."

He climbed into the truck giving her a wave.

She waved back as he drove away, she took a few minutes to compose herself before she went to find Kane.

'What the hell.'

She was more than taken aback to see the launch's return and to see Kane on the dock getting on board and leaving.

He didn't even say goodbye. 'Well, that sucks out loud.' And she felt incredibly hurt.

As she walked into the cabin, her phone was ringing, she didn't recognize the number but answered anyway.

Without even waiting for her to say hello he started talking. "Becca, apparently they've been trying to reach me all morning. Major issue in the engine room so I'm heading back to the yacht. I don't know how long I'll be… we may have to wait until tomorrow for our shopping trip. I'm so sorry sweetheart please don't be mad. I'll be back as soon as I can."

She didn't have much to say, she felt ill. Really ill.

She managed an 'okay' and 'no worries' and hung up.

She made it into the bathroom just in time to throw up breakfast and her meds. And thought… 'Maybe that third cup of coffee wasn't the best idea.'

After brushing her teeth, she went and laid down for a little while.

Her head hurt and she was feeling really sick.

After a few more trips to the bathroom and dealing with a couple of bouts of dry heaves she managed to sleep for a good two hours.

Once awake and noting that Kane was still gone, she went and got some water, happy that it stayed down but really wished she had a Propel or PowerAde since the thought of actual food sounded horrible and instantly made her nauseous.

Still, she was well aware that she needed to get something in her system since all the signs were there for low blood sugars.

Minor shakes and a major headache were always a tell.

Just the thought of eating food gave her another bout of dry heaves, she did have that small bit of water.

*Well, not any more.*

She went and got a bowl to put by the bed since she was feeling very drained and didn't know if she'd make it to the bathroom the next go round.

Once she rested and suffered another bout of dry heaves, she called Jake since she couldn't call Kane; she'd murdered his phone the day before.

"Hey, Aunt Bec's, what's up?" He always sounded so cheerful when he spoke to her.

She really did love the boy.

"Are you on the water today with Justin?" She knew she didn't sound right, and he'd pick up on that.

"No, it's our day off. What's wrong Becs?" He went from cheerful to cop sounding concerned.

"Sick," she dropped the phone. "SHIT."

"I'm on my way Becs. Do you need to go to the hospital?" Yep, cop mode.

"NO! Flu Jakey… just needed something with electrolytes like zero PowerAde but you're not on the water so never mind." She couldn't remember ever feeling so tired.

"Screw that Becca… I'll be there in thirty. And where the fuck is Curt?" Now he sounded like his father.

"Gone." She didn't have any strength to explain.

She didn't mean to hang up, but she was back asleep before the phone hit the floor.

Truth was she passed out cold.

"Aunt Becs!" Jake raced in the cabin.

She was groggy when he stormed in the bedroom.

"What the hell Jakey… why you shouting?" Her look of confusion and coloring stopped him dead in his tracks.

"Becs, you look so pale." He handed her a bottle of PowerAde.

She sat up and took a good long drink. It tasted amazing and she was glad it was nice and cold.

She heard the siren.

"You little shit... you called the EMTs?" She took another drink as Justin came in.

"You look like hell Becca. Is it your blood sugar? Do you need some fruit juice?" He looked as concerned as Jake.

"How *Steel Magnolias* of you and NO! I have a flu bug. Overreact much JJ?" But she couldn't be too mad since she knew they did it out of love. And she really appreciated the cold drink they had brought.

The EMTs had arrived in her bedroom.

'It's a party now.' She just shook her head.

"Where the fuck is Curt?" Jake was a tad miffed when he asked.

The EMTs were taking vitals and testing her sugar levels so she wasn't supposed to talk, and she gave her nephew a 'wait a minute' look.

When they finished, she told her nosy nephew that he got another call back to that yacht of his and she wasn't sick when he left so he had no idea and reminded Jake that his phone was no longer operational.

"Shit, I forgot about that. Okay, we can fetch him from Hope if you want us to?" He was trying to make amends for snapping at her.

She really loved the overprotective little shit. But shook her head.

"Ma'am your blood pressure is low, your pulse is a bit weak, and your sugars are way too low, we need to get an IV going. We'd like to get you to the hospital if you're agreeable." EMT one was trying to be helpful.

"It's just the flu for heaven's sake. I don't think I really need to be rushed to the hospital." She looked at her nephew.

He asked the EMTs if he could take her?

EMT two was the senior officer and said it would be best if she went with them since they wanted to put the IV in before they left.

They all turned when Kane burst into the room.

'FUCK, now it really was a party.' She would have laughed if she had the energy. Her eyelids again had a mind of their own and she felt as though she'd fall asleep without any warning at this point.

At least the PowerAde was staying down. Small favors.

"What the hell is going on? Becca, are you okay?" His voice was a bit on the frantic side.

Jake filled him in on everything the EMTs had said, and he told them to take her.

"Hey, I think I should have a say…" but her voice trailed off at the end. Her earlier thoughts were correct, no warning.

"Take her now! Aunt Becs we'll meet you at the hospital." Jake didn't think she heard him.

Becca woke to a buzzing sound and tried to hit the snooze button, but her arm was attached to something.

She opened her eyes to find herself in the hospital.

"FUCK me! REALLY!" She hated hospitals.

Her mom died in one and so did Mary.

She heard Kane chuckle. He was holding her hand and she didn't even see him, distracted by the IV in her other arm.

"You get a pass on that one sweetheart." He leaned up and gave her a kiss.

"Why am I here? Will you please get me out?" Her eyes were pleading.

"No. You have a really bad flu bug and need to get some fluids and medication in you to keep your sugars up. But you should be able to go home tomorrow." He was kissing her hand.

She whispered, "People die in hospitals." And the tears were streaming down her face. It was her one true fear.

"No, sweetheart don't… it's just a flu bug I swear. I promise I'll get you out of here as soon as they say it's okay." He was wiping away her tears and kissing her cheek.

Hospitals are busy places and she nor Kane had noticed the arrival of another until he spoke, startling them both.

"Mrs. Jackson, I'm Dr Lee." Noticing her tears, he asked if she was in pain.

She shook her head and Kane told the doctor she didn't like hospitals.

"No one does, but you're going to be fine. I want to give you one more bag of fluid and a bit more nausea medicine and I think you can go home. I don't see any need to keep you overnight." He smiled and got a huge smile back from Becca. And with that he took his leave.

Kane was looking down at his phone. "I'll text Jake the news. He went to pick up a few protein drinks and more zero PowerAde."

"You have a phone?" She cocked her head.

"Your nephew is very hard headed. He refused to bring me to the hospital until I got a new phone. And truth is, I was grateful since I never want to find you like that again. You should have been able to get a hold of me." He sighed.

"Becca, you scared the shit out of me. I would die if something happened to you. I love you." He leaned in and gave her another more intimate kiss.

She was crying again... happy tears. 'He said it first, again.'

"I love you too Kane. So very much. But stop kissing me, I don't want you to get this crap."

"In sickness and in health woman." And kissed her again.

She had the biggest smile on her face but was having issues keeping her eyes open. 'Not again. Fuck.'

It was only an hour later when she woke up but this time, she actually felt... good. Her head didn't hurt any longer, she didn't feel nauseous, and she felt fully rested. 'Wow.'

She was, however, alone in her room. 'Where was Kane?'

A few minutes later Jake walked in and gave her a nice kiss on the cheek.

"You look a hundred times better Aunt Becs. Please don't scare me like that again. I'm a bit young for gray hair."

Yep, he had his dad's smile.

She asked the one question that most mattered at that precise moment. "Where's Kane?"

"Becca, who the hell is Kane?"

Her breath caught and she went ashen.

"Oh shit, you mean Curt. Sorry, he went to take a call and to use the bathroom. Why do you call him by his last name?" He looked highly perplexed at her reaction.

Before she had a chance to explain the name thing, Kane came back in her room, so Jake excused himself.

"Sweetheart, you look pale again. How are you feeling?"

She grabbed him and gave him a huge hug, only relaxing when he was closer.

He stroked her hair and kissed her forehead.

"What's going on?" He was regarding her with more than a little curiosity.

The nurse interrupted them and took out her IV letting her know that the doctor had discharged her but if she started to feel worse to come right back. She also handed Kane a prescription for anti-nausea medicine to be taken as needed.

As soon as Becca was free from her tether she asked for her clothes and went into the bathroom, which she desperately needed after all that IV fluid.

She came out dressed but was told she had to wait for an orderly to bring a wheelchair… hospital policy.

She looked quite despondent.

To somewhat appease her, Kane pulled her into another hug, and she melted into his embrace.

The world seemed so much better, with him near.

Jake was waiting for them in his truck, after a quick trip to the pharmacy.

*Okay, quick being comparative. But it did help that Jake knew practically everyone in the small town.*

He ran them back to the cabin in his boat… fifteen minutes as opposed to forty. Hell Yeah!

*And before you even ask, yes, she was forced to wear a life jacket but when Kane tried to pull that bullshit on Jake, he got a firm 'NO'.*

Jake shook his head when he saw his aunt wearing one.

She rolled her eyes at him, and he laughed.

"I saw that Becca and my rules still stand." he gave her a knowing smile and a wink.

She put her head on his shoulder and told him to 'lighten up' she'd had a very trying day. He nodded.

When Jake pulled up to the cabin, everything looked the same. She almost laughed at herself. Why wouldn't it... she'd only been gone six or seven hours.

He handed Kane his cooler and said he'd pick it up the next day when he and Justin were back on the water, officially.

He gave his aunt a huge hug. "Please don't scare me like that again Aunt Becs."

With a wave and 'love you' he set off back towards town.

Kane took her hand and led her up to the cabin. She wondered if he'd let her take a quick dip in the lake.

Not on your life was a definite negative on that thought.

"Becca, I want you to go change into pajamas and get in bed. I'll bring you a shake in a minute." He was putting the contents of the cooler in the fridge.

When she walked into the bedroom, she noticed the puke bowl from earlier and took it out the back door to wash in the lake.

"REBECCA LYNNE, WHAT THE FUCK ARE YOU DOING?"

'WOW, he seriously overreacts sometimes.' She shook her head holding up the now clean bowl.

That did not change his very angry face. Nope, not one bit sexy.

Damn scary actually.

She walked up the stairs to face his wrath with her best 'I'm sorry' face and to her surprise he just pulled her into a hug.

"Don't leave without telling me please. I would have cleaned the bowl. Now back to bed before I forget you're sick." Giving her a light smack on the ass.

She hugged him back and did as she was told.

# TUESDAY

Becca woke early the following morning having to pee, again. 'Fuck.' She'd already been three times during the night.

But then again, Kane made her drink not one but two shakes throughout the evening, another PowerAde and two bottles of water.

Her system was thoroughly flushed, that's for damn sure.

He also insisted on escorting her the first time in case she was shaky.

'What a sweet man, even if he was a tad overbearing.'

She got up without disturbing the beautiful caregiver next to her and headed out to the bathroom.

She was feeling almost a hundred per cent recovered but thought better of having any coffee.

She managed to get a fire going without too much difficulty.

It started to warm up the chilly cabin almost immediately.

She then went and tested her numbers.

Well, considering her lack of food the day before, they didn't totally suck.

She filled a cup with water and put in the microwave to heat, tea would be nice since she wanted something warm.

She was just throwing the teabag in the trash when Kane flew by her, and she heard him puking in the bathroom.

'Damn it, I gave him the flu, well shit.' She just shook her head.

Seeing her beloved was sick, it made her wonder about her brother since she didn't have her phone the better part of yesterday, she went to see if he texted her.

He had.

*Home safe but puked most of the way. Not a fun day.*

*Hope you don't get this shit.*
*Love you, James*

While Kane was still indisposed, she texted her nephew to see if he was sick too.

She smiled when he texted back:

*Hell no, healthy as a horse.*

Kane came out looking pale and she went and got him a clean pair of sweatpants she found while rummaging in the dresser a few weeks back.

More than likely belonging to her nephew.

Once he was in fresh clothes, she put him back to bed with her former puke bowl.

She rubbed his back until he was fast asleep.

She took that opportunity to sanitize the bathroom and hand wash his pajama bottoms.

She liked taking care of him.

Not wanting him sick but tit for tat considering what she put him through.

She called Jake and asked if he'd bring fully sugared PowerAde and some chicken noodle soup to her when he came by for his cooler and in turn, she'd have lunch packed and ready for both him and Justin.

Oh yeah… he loved that barter.

She was sitting next to Kane when he woke and handed him a cool glass of ice water and one of the anti-nausea pills, they had gotten the day before.

He didn't argue and laid his head in her lap after swallowing the medicine.

"I'm so sorry I made you sick." She was stroking his back.

She thought he might have said 'me too' before he fell back to sleep.

She remembered that was all she wanted to do yesterday… this flu really did knock you on your ass.

'How in the hell did James drive over eight hours with it.' Her brother never ceased to amaze her.

When he shifted his head, she moved and went to finish packing up the boys' lunch since she saw their boat heading her way.

She met them on the dock and handed Jake back his 'Yeti', which contained their lunch and in turn she took the sack of drinks and soup.

She'd also put thirty bucks in the cooler to pay him back but knew better than to tell him since she was also aware that the stubborn little shit would try and return it to her.

That trait ran throughout the family line.

"Thanks Jake, Kane is sick now and from my understanding so is your dad."

"Yep, you can thank Mark's kids... they all have it, so my guess is he'll be canceling their outing tomorrow." He shrugged.

"Probably for the best... I'm just glad you didn't get it." She smiled at her favorite nephew.

She loved his brother as well, but Mark was always distant. Even if they were in the same room. Over shadowed by his little brother.

"See you later Aunt Becs, love you and we'll come by Saturday for the official goodbye." His fake pout made her laugh. He was taking her to the airport on Sunday.

*Yep, her favorite.*

With bag in hand, she headed back inside to check on her patient.

He was sitting up drinking a bit of water.

"Would you like a nice cold PowerAde? Or maybe a protein shake?"

He passed on the shake but drank a whole bottle of PowerAde.

She also managed to get some chicken soup into him and another anti-nausea pill before he took an early afternoon nap.

At that point, it occurred to her that she'd not eaten anything either and downed a shake while cleaning up the few lunch dishes.

As predicted, Mark called and canceled the next day's visit with major apologies for getting her sick.

"Shit happens nephew... the joys of having kids. We're good by the way." She hoped he could feel her smile through the phone.

She also told him to check on his dad too since he also got the flu, and she would see him the next year.

He told her that he would be coming out Saturday afternoon with Jake. The kids may not but he was not going to wait a year to see her.

That made her heart feel better.

Just as they were saying their goodbyes, Kane's phone started ringing.

She walked it into the bedroom, but he was still fast asleep. She just let it go to voicemail.

When the same number called a few minutes later she thought it might be important, so she answered it.

"Hello... who's this... I see... just a minute please." She hit the hold button and walked into the bedroom and threw the phone at him.

He woke with a start. "What the hell Becca?" He saw his phone and her face.

"Your girlfriend is on the phone." She spat it out like something vile had crawled into her mouth.

"No, she's not... she's standing in front of me looking really pissed."

Becca turned to leave.

"SIT YOUR ASS DOWN!"

That made her jump and do what he said. 'Wow he's still scary when he shouts. Even when sick and in bed. Damn.'

It was his turn to look miffed.

He hit the hold button to release the call and put it on speaker so Becca could hear the whole conversation.

"Hello." His voice was stern.

"Hi Curtis, where are you? I went by the house and the boatyard, but no one would tell me anything. We need to talk. And who answered your phone baby?" She had a very sing song delivery... Becca hated her instantly.

"What the hell could we possibly need to talk about Teri. We haven't spoken or seen each other in well over a year. I believe you were fucking that bartender behind my back the last time I saw you." He motioned for Becca to come closer.

She did and he wrapped her in his arms and kissed her cheek as they both waited for her response.

"I made a mistake Curt. I want to make it up to you. I want us to try again. Can I see you? This is hard over the phone." She was crying.

Becca rolled her eyes and Kane smiled.

"Not interested. Moved on and it was my fiancée that answered our phone. So 'no' to everything you asked. Don't call me again." And with that he hung up.

Becca looked utterly shocked...she'd never seen him be cruel and she also knew he used the other 'f' word for effect, but it had an effect on her too.

She turned and gave him a very passionate kiss.

"Well, well my beautiful girl, I never thought that you would or could be so jealous. I like it. But I am feeling too weak to do much more than return your very welcoming kiss." He was caressing her cheek.

"I'm okay with that. I'll get you some more ice water. Do you want any food?" She was back to nurse mode.

He shook his head and wrapped his arms around her not letting her leave his side.

She now knew that he'd been hurt by that woman, and it took him over a year to heal. Maybe they had more in common than she thought.

She relaxed in his loving arms and laid down beside him.

They both took a late afternoon siesta.

When she woke, the sun had moved to the west but still had a couple hours of light left and Kane was caressing her ass.

That man could turn her on so easily.

"Kane, you're sick, what do you think you're doing?" Her body shuddered at his touch.

"Get naked woman... do it now." And slapped her ass, hard.

'OH MY!'

She could tell he wasn't up to his normal stamina but even a quart low his vitality was amazing, and he left her fully satisfied and then some.

They were laying in each other's arms enjoying the after effect of making love when he asked about the plan for the next day. She told him that Mark had to cancel since it was the kids who shared the lovely flu bug with everyone, including James.

"So, tomorrow is open then?" And he got a huge grin.

She nodded and asked what he had in mind.

"Rules woman. And shopping. But first, would you please heat up some more of that wonderful soup."

"Of course." And with that, gave him a quick kiss, grabbed her robe and went to make her man some dinner.

She returned twenty minutes later with a lap tray so he could sit up and eat. He got a heartier version of chicken soup, toast, crackers and another ice-cold PowerAde.

She covered all the bases. 'Thank you, Jake.'

He managed to eat a few crackers and almost all the soup and then asked what she'd eaten that day.

'Well shit.' She confessed to only two protein shakes and her last PowerAde, he informed her that wasn't nearly enough food for the day.

"Becca, please go fix yourself something for dinner. I want you to stay healthy. You're going to need your strength for the rest of this week."

His wink was felt all through her body.

'DAMN!'

She had been sitting on the other side of the bed, keeping him company while he ate and when she came around to pick up the tray, Kane moved it out of reach to the side she just vacated.

He then slowly stroked her leg, starting at the back of her thigh and moving up.

"What do you think you're doing? You need to rest and as you just stated, I need to go fix my dinner." Becca went to move but his arm wrapped around her legs.

He shook his head and continued his upward sensual assault. Her breathing was getting raspy as he made short work of turning her on. Again.

"Who doesn't like getting dessert first sweetheart?" And in one fluid motion he opened her robe and slid his fingers inside her as his lips, teeth and tongue got her nipples nice and aroused, she moaned her approval.

It was erotic and her release felt amazing at the hands of her love.

He pulled Becca onto the bed next to him.

"I don't think you're done yet." He gave her a very passionate kiss and made sure she exploded a second time before she had even come down from the first one.

Becca whispered, "No more, please."

She was still trying to catch her breath and slow her heart. Wrapped in his arms with those amazing hands caressing her back.

"Thanks for taking care of me today. Just wanted to return the favor."

She managed a very quiet, "Welcome." She was fast asleep minutes later.

Becca woke two hours later after her hand hit the soup bowl and the spoon went flying somewhere in the dark.

Kane was snoring softly.

'I need to get an 'out of service' sign for my vagina.' That thought made her chuckle.

Softly since she didn't want to disturb her wonderful man.

She got up as quietly as she could and took the tray into the kitchen.

Minus the spoon which she couldn't find without turning on the light.

She grabbed the robe she was wearing and threw it into the dirty clothes and selected a pair of shorts and oversize T-shirt before walking naked through the cabin and into the bathroom.

After a quick shower she emerged in her sleeping attire and cleaned up the dinner dishes.

She also ate a yogurt, her version of supper since it was getting too late to have anything more substantial.

She then went and found a tumbler with a lid and made a PowerAde with ice for Kane in case he woke thirsty.

'What can I do for this wonderful man? Some way to thank him?' Her smile got huge when the light bulb finally went off.

A small voice reminded her that she was very bad at oral sex, but she was going to learn to do it right, for him.

A wayward thought had come and gone but left her with that strange feeling again. 'Been here done that'.

Yep. Freaking Fucking Tuesday! AGAIN!

After locking up the cabin and putting the drink on Kane's bedside table Becca climbed under the sheets for a good night's rest.

Even in his sleep his arms encased her.

She was head over heels in love with this man.

# WEDNESDAY

The sun was barely up when Becca opened her eyes. She felt well rested and very hungry.

Kane was still asleep, and she remembered her special thank you idea.

'Come on Becs, put your big girl panties on and get this show on the road.' Good pep talk. And oddly familiar. Jeez, again.

She was glad he slept on his back for the most part. This would have been a much bigger challenge if he slept on his side or stomach.

She was also glad he was sleeping in the nude.

'He's huge… I hope I don't dislocate my jaw.' That thought gave her some nervous giggles and she again had to admonish herself.

*Anxious doesn't even begin to describe what she was going through.*

She slid down under the sheets and slowly caressed his penis, first with her fingers and then started to give it kisses. But it didn't come fully alive until her tongue started licking the shaft and she heard his moan.

'No time like the present.'

She wrapped her lips around his now fully erect appendage and slowly brought as much of it as she could into her mouth.

She pushed down as it went in and sucked as she pulled it out finding a rhythm that she hoped he'd find enjoyable.

His moans told her that whatever she was doing, was pleasing him.

Now awake. "Oh, fuck, that feels amazing."

She was so happy and ran her teeth ever so gently down his shaft on the next pass and his moan was even louder.

"Becca, you need to stop before I come." He was breathless.

She knew the feeling.

Getting back to the task at hand she kissed the tip his penis and ran her tongue up and down the shaft again before letting her mouth have its fun.

His moans were getting more erratic, and she knew he was close to his release.

"Becca stop… I'm going to come."

She had other ideas and with determination she went down twice more and tasted his salty release, savoring it as it went down her throat.

She'd done it… 'YES!' She kissed his penis once more before she crawled out from under the covers.

His look was one of being loved and she smiled at him. She knew that feeling too.

"That felt so wonderful and you're a natural my girl. Whoever told you that you weren't, was a complete idiot." That smile said it all for her.

When his hand made its way down her back towards her ass, she stopped him. "This morning was about you. I wanted to do something special for you." She put her lips to his and gave him a very tender kiss.

"I love you Kane."

She started to get up and he had her back in a lip lock before she had one foot out of bed.

His tongue found hers and pretty soon they were both moaning.

He pulled her shorts off and slid deep inside her.

"It's not about me or you… it's about us. And I love you too."

That morning they even climaxed at the same time.

She was cooking them breakfast and remembering every kiss, every caress and the feeling of him deep inside her. It was glorious and she knew she'd never get enough of him.

All her thoughts of 'out of service' were long gone.

"Over thinking baby?" He smiled at her as he came in looking fully recovered. She shook her head.

"Just remember how wonderful you feel inside me." She blushed as she said it.

He wrapped his arms around her.

"Oh, we'll be doing that again and soon. But first, feed me woman, I'm starving." And with a quick slap on her ass, he went and sat at the table.

She put two slices of French toast on his plate, along with over easy eggs and both bacon and sausage.

She had eggs, sliced tomato and a piece of bacon. Well two since Kane put another one on her plate.

"Eat everything Becca… you didn't eat nearly enough yesterday and today you are going to need your strength." And again, the wink that resonated throughout her whole body.

DAMN! REALLY!!

With the kitchen cleaned and both she and Kane well nourished, she went and made the bed while he was taking a shower.

'There's that stupid spoon.' She laughed.

She was glad that flu bug was only twenty-four hours and that she didn't get any relapse from her and Kane's activities the day before.

She took five minutes to call James and make sure he was doing better, and he was.

Apparently, he was down for two days but then again, he drove for eight hours and didn't give his body a chance to recover.

He also let her know that the kids and Mark were feeling better as well but Amy had it now.

Oh Yeah. That actually made her smile.

Becca made an art form out of grudge holding.

She said her 'love you's' and goodbyes and went to take her turn in the shower since a very naked Kane walked by her while she was on the phone.

AGAIN…WOOF! And DAMN!!

She changed in the bathroom after cleaning up and went ahead and used the blow dryer on her hair that morning. She had a feeling they might be heading to Spokane for a bit of shopping.

"You look beautiful Becca and smell divine. I really like that perfume. What is it?"

She told him it was in fact called 'Beautiful'.

"Very fitting. You look ready for our day out." He had a very interesting look on his face.

One that told her, he had a plan brewing in his mind and she may or may not like it.

"What did you have in mind Mr Kane?" Her look was much coyer.

Eyebrows raised. "Well, that is one option, but I think we'll go shopping today. And like Monday, the rules are back in place for the next eight hours. Do you remember what they are?" Wicked grin.

She nodded but didn't smile.

Cabin locked up, purse over her shoulder and Kane holding her hand, they headed up to the Enclave.

*It had been her mom's car and now considered the cabin car. Becca was the one who used it the most, but it was available to any family member. Jake kept it in his garage during the winter months and kept up with its maintenance.*

When Kane reached for the passenger door it was still locked. He looked at her with a puzzled expression and she grinned.

"I think I'd like to drive. It wasn't against any of your rules if memory serves." But his advancement was quick, and he had her pinned against the hood.

"Same as before woman, you drive, and I play with you... all of you." He was sucking her earlobe, which drove her crazy, so she handed him the keys but not before caressing his groin, ever so softy.

"Fine, you drive."

He growled at her and it took everything in her power not to roll her eyes.

They were twenty minutes into their drive before the sexual tension in the car subsided and Kane turned on the radio.

KPND-FM, classic rock. Nice. She grew up with that station.

"Becca, tell me about Mary? I want to know everything about your life. If you'd like me to know that is?" He was wearing her favorite smile. How could she refuse?

Still, Mary... hard subject that brought both happiness and a deep sadness.

She smiled at a memory and then began to talk.

"I was on my second or third day in Juneau, when we met. I liked her from the start. Mary was larger than life, carried herself as if she were above the crowd, not stuck-up mind you, but not getting bogged down with life's idiosyncrasies. We became friends that day. It must have been the following week that she informed me that we were going to be the very best of friends...

she was right of course. Within that year she was introducing me as her best friend in the whole universe. She was a force, and I was in awe of her. We were nothing alike." She paused thinking of something she didn't say out loud.

"When she got a job working for the Alaska tourism department, she traveled all over the state. Hell, all over the country. She loved meeting new people, seeing new towns and having new experiences. But no matter where she was, she'd call me every Sunday morning and we'd shoot the shit for a good hour or two. Not talking about anything earth shattering... just keeping our connection." She paused again, getting a drink of water.

Kane reached over and took her hand.

"My ex didn't like her, he would say she overshadowed me, and she did but I didn't care. The hypocrite was actually hitting on Mary when he and I met for the first time. I was used to playing second fiddle to her. I was definitely a beta to her alpha, for the first several years at least. But she always offered me unconditional love and support." She looked out the window for a minute or two. He squeezed her hand bringing her back to him.

"We went through so much together. Her divorce, her many break-ups that followed and the loss of her dad. It was years before mine."

She took a veer to tell him the 'joke' about the cat on the roof in a way of understanding the very dark sense of humor that Mary had.

*Oh, if you don't know it... it is so much better verbally. But here goes.*

*A guy has to go away on business and leaves his most prized possession, his cat, in the care of his sister.*

*When he calls later that evening to inquire about 'Mr. Snuffles' his sister tells him that he got hit by and car and is dead.*

*He's mortified and tells his sister that is no way to deliver shocking news.*

*He then informs her that she should have told him 'The cats on the roof and she was trying to get him down' and then the next day, she should tell him that 'the cat took a small tumble off the roof and was being looked after at the vet's office' and on the last day tell him 'his beloved feline passed away peacefully'. His sister told him she was sorry and would remember to be gentler the next time she needed to deliver bad news and he thanked her. Then he asked how their mother was doing. She paused, 'Mom's on the roof!'*

For some reason, Kane found that very funny and was laughing pretty good and asked why she had to stop and tell him that.

"Mary was living in Fairbanks, hell I moved her there. She needed a change after getting out of a bad marriage, so ten years after we met, I packed her car and put her and my ass on a ferry. I flew home once I had her settled. Anyway, about two years later I got a call and all she said was, 'My dad's on the roof'. I took the next flight out of Juneau to go and see her. I couldn't make the trip back east, but her sister was there and her two uncles so at least she had family. Her mom passed when she was still in middle school, so she was really tight with her dad, it was a very hard loss for both her and her sister."

Becca wanted to wrap this up, so she skipped the next decade.

"Mary was getting tired of the cold and moved to Vegas about two years before my mom got sick. When I called to tell her my, 'Mom was on the roof', she couldn't make the trip north. She made up some excuse. But like I told you before, she called me daily. It wasn't the same, but it was all she could do at the moment. I came to find out later that she was getting chemotherapy at the time. Yep, she hid that little chestnut." She was taking a few deep breaths.

"I told you this part about her encouraging me to find my life, my happiness since she knew deep down her life was coming to a close. And that's why she pushed me so hard to find work back in Alaska and also to get a divorce a year and a half later. She had a good twenty months before the cancer was back with a vengeance. It was the last two weeks of the first semester when she finally let me know how bad it was. She hadn't given me the choice to be there for her, not until the end. She at least called me in time so I could fly down and watch her die. One week before Christmas. That was just this past year." Tears were streaming down her face.

They were getting closer to Spokane, and she was done talking. She was just looking out the window. Letting that fissure in her heart have its moment.

She was in no mood to shop, and he picked up on that pretty quick.

"Becca, I'm sorry. I didn't want to upset you... I'm jealous as all hell that she got you for all those years. I wish it were me." He squeezed her hand.

Well, that's got to be one of sweetest things she'd heard, ever.

"Thank you. I wish that too." She truly loved this man.

"So, I have a surprise for you and it's not shopping. And considering that you've just had a very emotional hour, I'd like to give you some relaxation therapy." He was smiling her smile.

'What is he up to?' She looked at him with questioning eyes.

Kane pulled off the highway and made his way to West Summit Parkway and parked in front of 'Spa Paradiso'. He turned off the engine and came around to open Becca's door.

He took her hand and led her into the very ultra-modern and sleek building.

A very tall and lean young woman greeted them.

Kane told her that he made an appointment for the 'Simply Sensational' spa package for his girlfriend.

"Good choice sir, it's one of our most requested." She was far too perky for her own good.

At this point Becca was just staring in disbelief. She'd never had a spa day and what in the hell made him think she wanted one.

Plus, the overly attentive woman talking a mile a minute to Kane was pissing her off.

He squeezed her hand to bring her out of her head and shook his.

"Becca, we talked about the over thinking, and I would like to treat you to a few hours of pampering. Please don't be difficult about this." Back to stern but sexy.

"And pray tell, what will you be doing while I'm getting exfoliated and buffed?" Just a wee bit of sass to her tone.

Eyebrow up was not a good sign.

"I have a meeting to discuss the possibility of a two-boat build. I'll be back before you're thoroughly buffed."

She knew that look and he was done with any more arguments.

Of course, while he was gone, she could roll her eyes as much as she wanted and if she wanted to over think her brains out, so be it.

"Becca, rules!" Aw, the stern but not so sexy look was back.

She smirked not giving a fuck.

With a quick kiss, not letting it be anything more, she thanked him for her 'spa day'. Bit too much saccharine. Oops!

Yep, she rolled her eyes.

And laughed at his astonished expression.

'I broke every fucking rule, so there.' She really couldn't stop herself.

She turned to the woman. "So, where do we start my 'Simply Sensational' day?" Oh, yeah... sassy as hell.

Before she could follow the young lady... Kane pulled her back into his arms.

"You're trying to provoke me on purpose and there will be consequences. I can promise you that." He was speaking in harsh whispers.

She pulled away to look at his face. "Oh, lighten up. And good luck with your meeting." Then gave him a much nicer goodbye kiss.

She thought he might have growled again at her, but he was gone, and her day of pampering began.

'Oh joy.'

The massage was surprisingly wonderful, and it relaxed her more than she thought possible. She didn't care for the thirty-minute facial... it seemed like a bit much, but her skin looked radiant so whatever they did made her look a good ten years younger. She reconsidered her first thought.

Never in a million years did she think she'd have a good time getting hot stones massaged into her calves. WRONG… it was heaven.

She really would have to thank Kane for the last couple hours.

As the hot towels were put on both her legs, the manicurist came and started working on her hands. Her name was Raven and she had purple hair and the nails to match.

She also had several piercings on her face and the most infectious laugh.

She spent the first half hour trimming, filing and taking care of Becca's horrid cuticles. She also tried to convince her to try a very outrageous color.

'NOPE!'

Disappointed that Becca wanted clear, she still managed to do a wonderful job on her nails and got her to add a little sparkle to both her fingers and toes.

The best part was the paraffin wax dip. It felt amazing and again seemed to make her hands look years younger.

Once done and feeling utterly pampered she made her way back out to the lobby where Kane was sitting.

"Did you enjoy yourself Beautiful?" And he was back to wearing her smile.

"Yes, very much and thank you." She walked right into his outstretched arms.

It was one of her favorite places to be.

She hugged him back and then asked about his meeting.

"It went great. We have the contract, and our deadline is next June to deliver." He was grinning from ear to ear.

"Let's go get some lunch or did they feed you here?" He pulled away to look at her.

She sighed since they offered a few times and she declined, only accepting water.

She shook her head.

He took her hand and looked at her nails. "Good, we can eat before we shop. No color? Nice sparkle though." He shook his head.

She rolled her eyes and thought she should introduce him to Raven if he wanted color.

"Saw that Becca. I'm keeping track."

Well of course you are... 'Mr. Quirky.'

On the way to the car, he had his arm around her at the waist and she had her head cradled into his shoulder. So much more intimate than just holding hands.

This was turning out to be a really good day.

When they pulled up near Clinkerdagger's, Becca smiled. She loved this restaurant. She and her mom had gone there a few times when they went shopping in Spokane for school clothes or a girl's day out.

Nice memory.

Its full name used to be Clinkerdagger, Bickerstaff and Petts; it was a mouthful, but she'd always liked the name.

Now of course it was just a restaurant and bar but still a great place to dine and walking distance to River Park Square and ample shopping.

She took his hand after he opened her door. 'Nice planning Mr Kane,' just a passing thought. No over thinking.

"After lunch I thought we might walk around the square to see if we can find you a few things." Such a hopeful look.

'Yep, totally planned this.' And she narrowed her eyes at him.

"What?" He chuckled at her as he led her into the restaurant.

Once seated they made short work of ordering drinks, appetizers and meals in one fell swoop.

Time for a few answers from the very sneaking Mr Kane.

"Kane, when did you know about this business meeting of yours and plan my spa day? And what exactly am I missing in my wardrobe? I think you've spent quite enough money on me. So, on that note, may I please buy lunch?" She sipped the water the waitress had left them at their arrival.

"I got the call when you were in the hospital. While you were resting later that afternoon, I made the appointment at the spa for you. I had no idea I was going to get the flu so I had to scramble to get everything rearranged for today, after you told me Mark and the kids wouldn't be coming to the cabin. I sent emails getting my business meeting rearranged for today and checking with the spa to see if they had any openings for this morning as well, worked out nicely. Now, as for your wardrobe… Sweetheart, what don't you need? Nothing fits you right. So, we'll start with new lingerie and work our way throughout the stores until you have at least five new outfits. Two causal, two business and one for a night on the town." His smile was 'don't mess with me' on this subject.

The waitress was back with their drinks and appetizers.

She took a bite of her prawn cocktail. YUM!

Kane made short work of his steamed clams and took the last two prawns offered by Becca.

"That was really good. Oh, and to answer your last two questions, 'no I haven't and no but thank you'." And excused himself.

'Does he seriously think I can't buy clothes for myself? And I can afford my own lunch and his, for heaven's sake I have money. Should we have that conversation already?' She must have had a very perplexed look on her face since the waitress was back retrieving their plates and asked if she was all right.

"Yes, I'm fine thank you. Everything was delicious." And she smiled at the departing young woman.

Kane was back and gave her a nice kiss before taking his seat.

"Becca, your brother told me that you had no money issues and that you work for insurance and for something to do. So, I am aware you can afford your own clothes. But I would like to buy you a few things and I want you to let me." He winked at her and gave her his permafrost melting smile.

How in the hell did he know what she was thinking?

"Okay." She wasn't exactly smiling but she wasn't frowning either.

In the back of her mind, she was planning revenge on her overly chatty brother.

She wanted the two men to get along, not to have some major bounding experience with her as their main topic of conversation.

BUSTED!

"Over thinking again my girl. Your list is getting a bit long. At this rate you may not be able to sit for a day or two."

She couldn't tell if he was kidding. And just shook her head.

Thank God their meals arrived.

Distraction was a wonderful thing.

Kane ordered the fish and chips, and Becca got the Caesar salad with blackened chicken. It was her go to meal whenever she was out. She did opt for the starter size and not the meal portion.

Ever cautious about her food consumption.

They ate in silence for a few minutes.

"Would you like to try some of my fish, it's very good." He was holding out a forkful of the tempera coated white fish.

She shook her head.

His sigh was quite audible, and it was her turn to cock her head with a quizzical expression.

He smirked at her. "You are always so careful what you eat. I find it exhausting and all I'm doing is watching you. One bite isn't going to derail your diet. Which brings me around to that subject. I want you to stop. I like that you have a little meat on your bones. I like it a lot if you hadn't noticed."

'Diet', the one four letter word she hated. More than hated... despised would be a better description. Her appetite was gone instantly, and she pushed her plate away.

*We need to take another quick veer here to explain that growing up with excess weight caused issues.*

*Teasing of course because children can be wretched little fuckers, but it was her loving parents who thought that every mood swing was weight related.*

*Seriously, HORMONES of an adolescent girl and they went with that.*

*Anyway, the subject of dieting was brought up continually throughout Becca's teens and always during a meal, usually dinner.*

*They thought that she'd be happier if she was thinner. It became a problem, more mentally for her but she still went on every fad diet to appease them... commence the yo-yo.*

*Her brother was out of the house by this point. He'd see the results and after effects but always thought she did it on her own for some social conformity.*

*She developed a bit of self-hatred and low self-esteem.*

*Who wouldn't when your parents can't seem to love you as you are?*

*Drama Queen mentioned earlier.*

*Let's get back on track, shall we?*

Before he could even react, she excused herself and headed towards the ladies' room. En route she gave her credit card to the waitress and asked her not to bring the check to the table.

Once refreshed, she signed the slip and gave the accommodating young lady a rather nice gratuity.

'Damn, with tip and tax, their lunch was a hundred bucks. No wonder her mom always called it a huge treat to eat there.' She smiled again at the fond memory.

Back at the table Kane was finishing up his meal and she sat picking up her iced tea.

He looked at her salad and her with a nod letting her know he wanted her to eat more.

"I'm good thanks. You ready to go?" She wasn't in any mood to shop, again.

"Just waiting on the check and we can leave." His look was more, 'What in the hell just happened?'

"All taken care of." And she was on her feet and heading for the exit.

He caught up with her in two good strides and took her hand to slow her progress.

As they walked out of Clinkerdagger's you could cut the tension with a knife.

Once outside she pulled her hand free from his.

They both turned on each other and said, "Listen—" at the exact same time causing them both to laugh.

*Mood changing laughter, the best kind.*

"Thank you for lunch Becca. May we please go and take a look around the square at least?" He was holding his hand out.

She nodded and put her hand in his.

*Good olive branch Kane. Well executed.*

They were wandering around Nordstrom's when he directed her towards the lingerie department.

He was nothing if not committed to his plan.

He held up a few teddies that left nothing to the imagination.

His smile was sinful and very seductive.

Becca just shook her head and thought, 'Not wearing that… it wouldn't look good for one and secondly the prices were stupid expensive.'

When the saleslady came and asked if they needed help, Kane told her that Becca would need to be measured to get the right size bra and could she also measure her waist for an accurate size for new panties as well.

That nearly floored Becca and she was having another very odd, 'been here done that' moment.

You guessed it, Freaking Fucking Wednesday!

"Would you excuse us for just a minute please." And with that he pulled her away from the woman to have a private conversation.

"Sweetheart, just appease me on this one issue. Well, this and one teddy, a couple of short nightgowns and the five outfits." He was whispering and blew into her ear making her body quiver.

"You cheat," she said and put her head on his shoulder. She also knew she'd do whatever he wanted.

"Yes, Beautiful, I do." His smile never left his face as he walked her back to the woman who now had two measuring tapes in her hand.

'FUCK.'

"Thinking it," she said and walked back towards the row of sleepwear chuckling.

'FREAK!'

When she came back out with her sizes written down on a piece of paper, Kane had an armful of clothing.

Note to self, 'NEVER, leave him alone in a lingerie department.'

He took the paper and handed her the stack of nightgowns.

He motioned to the sales woman that she'd need to try them on. But when he asked if she could show him, the woman told him 'No' and that put a HUGE smile on Becca's face.

'Serves you right.' She gave him a small wave as she headed into the dressing room.

She went through the stack and discarded three without taking them off the hanger.

'What the fuck was he thinking!'

She liked the navy-blue nightie with the deep neckline both in the front and back. It was flattering and sexy, even to her. That made her smile.

The white one was a bit see-through but fit nicely. She got that one for Kane. And the two satin short sets made the pile since the one she had was too big for her now.

She also gave in on one of the three black teddies since she didn't want to be there all night. The pink one got off the hangar but never got tried on. Again… what was he thinking?

'Five out of eleven… done.'

She hung up the six rejects to be put back by staff and emerged with the five. To her surprise or not, he had four bras picked out, a long dark maroon negligee and a dozen panties.

He didn't make her try any of those on and she liked three of the four bras and eight of the twelve panties made the cut. Thongs… NO!

She was not given a choice regarding the long nightgown.

The bill was still over seven hundred bucks and she wanted to put some more back but he told her, "Not on your life."

"I'm so looking forward to you modeling each and every one of these items for me." He winked and she had to catch her breath.

He had the bag in one hand and hers in the other and headed for women's clothing.

She was dragging her feet a bit.

"I know you're ready to go but indulge me for just a little longer please. I've already picked out a few items and they're in the dressing room waiting for you, but I will want to see them and was told I could by the nice young woman who works in this department." He gently squeezed her hand.

She gave in.

*Well of course she did. None of you should have doubted that.*

He'd been busy. Three pairs of jeans, two pairs of slacks, six shirts, four sun dresses and two evening dresses, one short and one long.

'This will take forever.' She sighed.

She tried on the slacks and instantly put one back. The other she let him see and he approved along with the top she'd chosen. She liked two out of three pairs of jeans and showed him two more shirts, one with each pair and got approval again.

'YES. Three outfits done.'

He only saw one dress and it did not meet with his arbitrary standards. Next thing she knew, the salesgirl was back with four more and took the rejects away.

After seeing two of the four, he nodded and that made five and she was done.

RIGHT?

NO!

"Cocktail dresses. Short one first and I'll wait right here."

'Stubborn jackass.'

She didn't like it but let him see it anyway and he nodded, and she shook her head.

The long dress didn't make it out of the dressing room.

Oh yeah, the girl was back with three more cocktail dresses and finally they both agreed on the same one.

Tired and cranky, Becca told him that she wanted to go home.

He teasingly asked about shoes and accessories.

Her look was almost violent.

"Just kidding, let me settle with the nice salesgirl and we can go." He put his hands up in defeat.

She gasped at the eleven hundred-and-seventy-three-dollar total, and he winked handing the young woman his credit card.

'Shit, he spent over two grand on me today.' She wasn't sure how she felt about that over extravagance.

"That was fun. Now let's get you home and naked." He didn't whisper that statement and both she and the young sales woman blushed.

Back in the Buick with purchases stowed he leaned over and gave her a very passionate kiss. One she felt everywhere.

"Wasn't kidding… I want you naked the minute we get to the cabin." One more quick kiss he started the car and headed for the highway.

DAMN!

She needed another distraction from her own body's needs and asked about the two boats he was commissioned to build.

He was animated and talked for the next hour plus about each of the boats. One was going to be owned by the head of the company but the second would be raffled off as a fundraiser with the proceeds going to at risk teens in eastern Washington.

"That is amazingly cool. I bet you gave them a special price on the second boat as your gift to the charity." She was beaming at her guy.

"Yes, 'Miss Psychic' I did." And brought her hand to his lips giving it a nice kiss.

"Can I ask you a very 'none of my business' question?" He nodded.

"How much does something like 'Daddy's Girl' cost?"

*Yes, she'd been wondering that since she saw the beast.*

"Our cost was about fourteen million to build her." And he waited for the second question.

Instead, she just nodded. 'Holy Fuck!'

"You surprise me Becca. Inquisitive but not intrusive. You are a rare find I must say." He was regarding her like a fine wine.

"Why thank you Mr Kane. You are constantly shocking the shit out of me." She was more whimsical.

He laughed.

"Not to ruin your mood but we need to discuss what happened over lunch. What did I say that put you off your food and well, me?"

He couldn't really look at her expression since he was going about seventy-five miles per hour on the highway.

She'd really hoped he's let that go since she did permit him to spend way too much money on her but there it was.

'Fuck, fuck, fuck.' She liked breaking his rules and smiled.

"Over thinking and dropping the 'f' bomb in your head... tsk, tsk, Becca."

"Whatever." And she rolled her eyes.

*Mentioned earlier she was a button pusher, do keep up.*

His lips were in a hard line, and she knew he wasn't happy with her.

'FINE! Jeez.'

"If you must know, I hate the 'd' word a zillion times more than you hate the 'f' word. Okay." Exasperated she put her head on the window and closed her eyes.

He reached over taking her hand back and bringing it back to his lips.

"I won't ever use that word again." He smiled her favorite smile.

She nodded and thanked him.

They were only a half hour away from the cabin and both their moods were suddenly better.

She finally felt relaxed.

It had been another roller coaster day when it came to mood swings.

"What would you like me to fix you for dinner this evening?" She wanted him talking again.

"Whatever you make will be perfect. But like I said earlier, you naked is first on my agenda."

She felt her heartbeat increasing.

There was tension between them again as he backed down the hill towards the cabin.

This time, it was sexual.

She got him talking the last twenty minutes of the drive and it was very titillating to say the least.

Not graphic mind you… he let her draw her own conclusions.

Becca found it quite stimulating all the same.

"Sweetheart, I think you should put on the black teddy… I never got to see you in it, and I would very much like to." He put the Enclave in park, reached back and grabbed a bag and handed her the article of clothing for which he spoke.

"Go! Now! I'll meet you there in a few minutes." His lustful growl got her moving down towards the cabin.

She didn't hate the teddy, but the back was a thong, and she wasn't used to that much skin showing. She turned around again, and this time Kane was in the doorframe.

"Me likes." And did a twirl with his finger.

She did as she was told.

He dropped all the bags and pulled her into his arms.

As his fingers moved up and down the sides of her new outfit, she shivered in anticipation.

He turned her around again looking at her exposed backside.

Without any warning his hand connected with a loud smack. He followed it with another and another.

"You broke the rules didn't you Becca."

She nodded.

"You were bad and bad girls get spanked, don't they?"

She nodded again.

"How many more do you think you deserve? You have to tell me, or I'll decide." His expression was primal again and he was arousing her not hurting her.

"Four." She knew it sounded weak and breathy, but she was on fire for him.

"Seems a little low but you've had four already. I think eight... we'll meet in the middle at six. Do you agree?"

She gave him a single nod.

He sat down on the bed and then pulled her down over his knee and gave her the agreed upon six arousing swats.

To his somewhat surprise, she attacked him, and he didn't seem to mind all that much.

Her body got the release it was craving at the skilled hands of her love.

"Damn woman, which was amazing. Let's do it again!"

She didn't have time to even react before he took possession of her lips, her breasts her entire body.

He's a force to be sure.

She loved how it felt having him deep inside her. It was the most powerful and sensual feeling.

She was cradled in his arms with her head on his chest listening to his heart, feeling completely satisfied.

"Thank you for this surprising and wondrous day. I loved it."

He was stroking her back.

"You are most welcome my beautiful girl, I did as well."

After a few more minutes of holding each other, she asked if he was hungry.

'Starving' was his exact word so she got up to fix dinner.

After he devoured two pork chops, scalloped potatoes and green beans, Kane relaxed in the living room while Becca got the kitchen tidied.

It was a lovely evening and perfect for a swim. She went and got her suit off the railing and changed before broaching the subject with 'Mr Phobia'.

"Kane, I'm going to take a quick dip in the lake." She was trying to sound nonchalant.

"Okay, but not past the dock please." His was very matter of fact.

She could live with that and agreed without a fuss.

Becca walked to the end of the dock and dove in making sure she was within the parameters of Kane's request. She didn't want to upset him.

She hadn't taken a swim in two days, and it felt so good, she decided to swim a lap or two down to the bunkhouse and back.

She loved to swim in the dark, it felt intimate and lovely.

He was calling her name when she was heading back from lap one. She waved and he started down towards the dock.

"How's the water?" He didn't look happy, but he was trying.

Bless his heart.

"Amazing, thank you." She stayed closer to shore with him on the dock.

She could see him relaxing right before her eyes.

"I was going to do another lap, or would you prefer if I got out of the water now?" She really was trying to keep the peace between them.

He requested the second option.

Well, she did get a little bit of a swim.

She walked out of the water at the shoreline, and he pulled her into his arms.

She tried to protest since she hadn't gotten her towel, but he wasn't letting her go.

When he finally released her, he told her to wait where she was and went and retrieved her towel from the end of the dock.

He had her hold it lengthwise in front of her. Not close enough to touch her body.

Not exactly an efficient way to dry off but apparently, he had other ideas.

He stood behind her and proceeded to remove her suit right there on the beach.

She tried to protest but his lips were on her earlobes, and she was feeling her desire building.

He tossed her suit at her feet and was caressing her now bare ass and kissing the nape of her neck.

"You drive me nuts when you swim in the dark so now it's my turn."

"I asked?" And when she tried to turn, she got a firm slap on his ass.

"Not the point woman, now keep those arms up."

His hands came around and started to play with her nipples as he continued nipping at her earlobes.

She leaned back into him, and he pushed her forward telling her not to move.

Her moans only fueled his seduction.

"Arms Up!" And he smacked her ass again.

His fingers moved south and were teasing her.

She wanted to move, to touch him but he warned her not to move again. Her breathing was becoming erratic as he slid his fingers inside her.

She gasped and came close to dropping the towel.

"Kane... please."

"Not yet, you need to be reminded that night swimming is to be done in the light of the cabin. Now, keep those hands or we're going to give some boater a nice floor show."

His fingers were keeping a steady tempo, his other hand was back pulling her nipples and his tongue and mouth hadn't left her earlobe or neck alone.

Her legs were feeling weak, and she knew her orgasm was close.

"Let go lover," was all he whispered, and she did.

He wrapped her in the towel and helped her up the stairs.

Jelly legs didn't even come close.

Once in bed he made short work of his clothes and slid deep inside her.

She screamed with her second climax, and he was just as vocal a few minutes later.

'DAMN, he really might kill me with orgasms.' She was smiling as sleep took her nestled in Kane's arms.

# THURSDAY

Becca woke the next morning feeling refreshed but alone. ODD.

The clock told her it wasn't quite seven. She debated for a few minutes whether or not to just stay in her warm cozy bed.

Nope, her bladder had other ideas.

She was naked and her robe was in the dirty clothes. 'Crap.'

She dug through the bag of lingerie and found one of her two new satin short and camisole sleep sets and put it on after removing the tags… the price still surprised her.

Shaking her head to dismiss the thought, she headed out into the main cabin and found Kane in the living room having a rather serious conversation on the phone.

Explained why he was not in bed when she woke.

He looked up and grinned at her making a twirling motion with his finger.

She didn't oblige him this time and headed straight in the bathroom.

Becca had other priorities at that moment in time.

When she came out, he was preoccupied with his phone call, so she went and got the coffee going and tested her numbers.

From Kane's side of the call, she gathered he was talking to Carl, and they were not in agreement about something.

She was glad he started a fire. The cabin was nice and warm, but she still felt a tad underdressed in her satin assemble. It didn't help that Kane was fully dressed in jeans and T-shirt.

She was wishing she'd thought to get a second robe while they were out shopping.

And then thought about getting in the shower and dressing before coffee.

In truth her thoughts were going down several bunny trails that morning, and she couldn't help but laugh at herself.

She also made a mental note that she'd need to do laundry as well. They'd managed to defile every king-sized set of sheets in the cabin. That thought alone made her blush. What fun that had been.

Tomorrow's chore list.

The boys would be coming out Saturday and they'd take whatever leftover food was in the fridge so she didn't have to worry about that, and Jake would drive them to the airport and take the Buick back to his place.

She'd have to remember to ask Jake if he wanted to stay in the bunkhouse Saturday night since she and

Kane now needed to be at the airport by eight a.m. on Sunday morning and that made for an early start.

She was brought out of her many, many thoughts when Kane raised his voice.

"DAMN IT CARL, this is getting really fucking old for me. FINE, but I swear it will be the last time or you can get your ass back here and deal with the idiot yourself."

He came into the kitchen after hanging up and took Becca into a huge hug.

"Want coffee?" She was gauging his mood for the day.

He hadn't let her go and shook his head as his hands moved down her back and landed on her ass.

His breathing started increasing as he stroked her satin shorts.

"Sweetheart, I am a fan of you in satin. Let's take this into the bedroom. Now please." He was removing her top before they left the kitchen.

She was catching her breath after their morning tryst. 'Holy hell, where did all his energy come from and could he bottle it, please?'

Okay... that seemed like another memorable thought. One that she was positive she'd had before. But when? Where?

Freaking Fucking Thursday.

He had her cradled in his arms and she could stay there all day; in fact, it was her favorite place to be, but she also knew they needed food.

Her numbers were good but with Kane's vigorous exercise schedule, nutrients were in order.

"What are you thinking about Becca?" he kissed her forehead.

"Food. And coffee actually." She smiled and kissed his lips.

"That sounds wonderful." And handed her back the satin short and camisole set.

She shook her head but put them back on since she didn't have a clean robe to put on. Mentioned on a few occasions now.

She was bending over looking into the fridge to see what all was left of the mountain of food they'd purchased the week prior.

He came up behind her reaching for a coffee cup and caressing her inner thigh.

"Mr Kane, kindly keep your hands to yourself. I'm trying to prepare your breakfast." She smirked at him.

He turned her around and pinned her to the fridge.

His lips parted hers so he could have full access and his hands were cupping her ass and pulling her as close to him as possible.

HOT. HOT. HOT!

He suddenly stopped. Released her and walked into the living room chuckling.

DAMN that man, he had her totally turned on. How does he just stop?

'REVENGE or food?'

She grabbed the ham, some cheese, mushrooms and eggs and decided a scramble was in order for the day.

She also popped in two slices of bread to toast for Kane.

While setting the table and drinking her coffee she came up with a plan for a bit of revenge.

First though, food, and she started by sautéing the mushrooms for a bit of color, followed by the ham and set them aside. She then whisked the eggs and cheese together and put them in the nice hot pan and pushed down the button on the toaster.

She flipped the egg concoction once and put the ham and mushrooms on the top with a bit more cheese and covered the pan and turned off the heat. Just needed to melt the cheese.

She then slipped into the bedroom to change... putting her flannel shirt over the top. It came down just low enough to cover her ass.

'Perfect.'

She plated his breakfast and hers, poured herself another cup of coffee and sat down before she called him to the table.

He looked surprised and disappointed that she was in her flannel shirt.

She feigned innocence.

"Looks delicious, thank you." He was still eyeing her wardrobe change with a bit of skepticism.

She told him he was welcome and doctored her eggs again with hot sauce and a bit of ketchup.

*Yep, he winced, again.*

She still didn't care, to her that was the only way to eat eggs.

He offered her one of his pieces of toast which she declined.

*None of you should have been surprised by that response.*

While busy eating he didn't seem to notice that every so often Becca undid a button on her flannel shirt.

She'd finished about two-thirds of her eggs and was done eating but did want more coffee.

As she stood, her shirt opened showing her very low-cut midnight blue nightie she'd changed into.

He dropped his fork.

"Oh, my bad." And started to button up her shirt.

"You little minx… don't you dare cover up." His voice was raspy, not quite the growl she was hoping for, but effective.

"Kane you sound a bit hoarse, I hope you're not getting sick again. I'll get you a cup of tea." And she turned around, grinning.

He grabbed the flannel shirt and slipped it off her shoulders exposing the back of the nightie which was also cut low exposing even more of her skin.

His fingers trailed down her spine giving her the shivers.

She turned and gave him a kiss taking her shirt back and walked into the living room, just as he'd done to her.

Actually, she went into the bathroom to brush her teeth and he cornered her in there.

He took her toothbrush, told her to spit and rinse and used it himself.

While he was attending to his dental hygiene, she managed to button up her shirt and was sitting on the couch when he came out.

"Bedroom Becca... and why are you back in that flannel shirt?"

She shrugged.

"I should do the dishes." And was just getting up.

He was shaking his head. "Think you're funny, do you? Getting me back for earlier? Two can play at that sweetheart."

And he took a seat on the couch and turned on the TV.

She smiled.

Walking by him, she hitched up the flannel shirt to expose her rather bare ass.

"Kiss this!" and RAN.

Nope, she didn't get the door shut or locked in time.

Sort of a win-win if you think about it.

Enjoying the after effects of their second morning tryst, Becca was laying on her stomach looking out at her lake with Kane's arm draped across her back.

She loved listening to his breathing while he slept. Very soothing.

And of course, she had to pee.

*Reality Bites!*

She started to wiggle out from beneath his arm which tightened around her. "Where do you think you're going woman?"

"Nature call." And tried to move again but he had her in his grasp.

"Which one?"

'RUDE question.' She did like a modicum of privacy… but the thoughts of everything else they'd done the past week flashed in her mind and made her laugh.

She told him she had to pee and let her up please.

He shook his head and got an evil smile; he then took her lips as his.

Her body's reaction was almost instant.

His assault was slow and methodical as he gave yet another release that morning but this one lingered as if you could feel it in the air.

She took the lord's name in vain a few times. But did mentally apologize to Kane's pastor brother.

He was smiling her smile. "Full bladders make for more intense orgasms."

'Damn straight!'

She wondered if there was a handbook with all this information and smirked at him.

She was just finishing up cleaning the kitchen by wiping down the table and saw a boat approaching.

It was the launch she'd seen several times before.

He never mentioned having to go back to 'Daddy's Girl'.

She then remembered his angry call with Carl, 'Last time or you come deal with the idiot'. HUH.

"Kane your ride is here." She then went back to her task and rinsed out the sponge.

He came and looked out the window. "What are they doing here? This was supposed to happen tomorrow. And yes…" looking into Becca's eyes, "I'm aware I didn't mention it. Still a bit pissed off actually."

He gave her a huge hug. "Sorry, but I will be as quick as I can and please don't swim without me here."

She shook her head.

Mr Phobia strikes again.

He followed his hug with a very nice kiss and headed down to the dock.

*Well of course she was tempted to put on her suit and dive in, have you not been paying attention?*

*She likes breaking rules. Especially stupid ones.*

Becca's phone rang as she watched and waved to the launch as it headed back towards Hope.

"Hello… Hi Mark… really… well that's great… yes of course, looking forward to it… sure… love you too… bye." She couldn't help but smile.

He was trying to suck up a bit since he'd ignored her the entire six weeks, she'd been at the cabin, and she was in fact leaving in just two and half days.

Still, she loved him and his kids, but his dingbat wife could and should stay the fuck away from her.

'NO RULES today!'

But with spankings like his… she would be fine being punished, anytime.

Back to the situation at hand. With Mark and the kids coming out the following day, she'd need to head to town and do laundry and pick up a few things more kid friendly in the food department.

'Oh shit.' And tell Kane where she'd be if he got back before her.

She tried to call but got his voicemail and told him to read his text message. Then typed a very lengthy text explaining what the new schedule was and of course letting him know she went to town.

Quick shopping list, laundry, six water jugs, purse, keys. 'Wow, I get to drive.' And locked up two of the three doors so Kane could still get back inside. She added that tidbit to the text as well.

She felt a twinge of sadness that she didn't have company on her trek to town.

'Come on Becs, make the best of it.' And with that, she plugged in her iPod and cranked the music nice and loud and headed up the hill.

Just getting into 'It's My Life' by Bon Jovi, her phone started to ring. She turned down the music. The car had Bluetooth, but she still hadn't set it up on her phone.

"Hello…? Hi Kane… just getting ready to turn onto the highway… hands free." She rolled her eyes, little white lie.

"Oh... no, I'm heading to the laundromat first... I can do that... yep... I'll wait for your call... love you too."

She turned the music back up and continued to sing along with Jon Bon Jovi all the way to town.

Once there she stopped at the first gas station to top off the tank.

Second stop was to get the laundry going.

'SHIT.' It was packed and yes, there was more than one, but this was her favorite.

She decided to do something she'd never done before and paid to have them wash her bedding, towels and bits of clothing. That way she could go do the grocery shopping before heading to city marina and picking up Kane.

Before she left, she filled the six water jugs.

*That's why he called earlier, letting her know that the launch would bring him to town so he could meet up with her.*

*So sweet.*

Her idea was to get everything she could bought and paid for before he called to let her know he'd arrived.

Hence stopping for gas.

He'd spent more than enough money this past week.

She raced through the store to pick up kid friendly food and was in checkout when her phone rang: Kane.

She smiled.

"Hi...? Okay... I'll get there in a few." She made it short since it was one of her pet peeves when people were on the phone in checkout lines. Very discourteous in Becca's opinion.

Kane was waiting at the top of the ramp for her, so she didn't even need to park but got out and gave him a nice kiss before letting him open the passenger door for her.

"Thank you for picking me up. Where to?" He was wearing her favorite smile.

"Laundromat, and back to the cabin." She was quite proud she got it all done in such a short amount of time.

"You're quick and I see you even filled the tank."

She nodded.

"Let's get lunch and then we'll pick up the laundry." He squeezed her hand.

How could she refuse that handsome face?

She nodded again.

During lunch he told her that the yacht had a glitch somewhere between the engine room and the bridge and he wasn't able to track it down. Carl would be coming back that night and they both had to spend time on 'Daddy's Girl' the next day to find the issue. He was hoping it would be a quick fix but just didn't know for sure.

"Is Carl hauling your boat all the way back here or is the launch picking you both up? Would you like him to stay in the bunkhouse?"

She hated that he'd miss meeting Mark and the kids, but she understood that his creation needed his attention.

"That is so very kind of you to offer but I don't want to share you with anyone for the rest of the day. He and Warren are bringing my boat back and will pick me up in the morning."

She was pleased beyond pleased with that bit of information. She didn't like to share him either.

Once Kane settled the lunch tab, they headed for the last stop before home.

Becca pulled out cash to pay for the laundry and Kane asked if she'd let him pay.

He got a resounding, "Not this time, I've got it." And he gave her his best pouty face. Didn't even phase her... for once.

When Becca came back out with the clean and bundled laundry, Kane was sitting in the passenger seat but made sure the back hatch was open for her.

'What the fuck is he up to now?' She eyed him wearily.

Climbing back in the driver's seat, she asked, "You're letting me drive, really?"

He nodded.

"Why?" She wasn't about to let this go.

"You've emasculated me, so you can just drive, and I'll sit here." He was actually sulking.

For some reason Becca found that highly amusing.

A very crass and rude thought went through her mind.

She was actually laughing by the time she pulled out of the parking lot.

"What may I ask is so funny? I'm up for a good laugh about now." He looked somewhat miffed.

She shook her head since it was really tactless. And she blushed.

"Becca, if you're laughing at me... don't you think I have the right to know what it's about?" Less miffed and more curious.

"My dear Mr Kane, I have found humor at your expense several times over the past week. Have you not been paying attention?" She smirked.

He laughed.

Finally!

"Pull over woman and let me drive before I do unspeakable things to your breasts." She did. His mood improved instantly, or at least it appeared to.

Back at the cabin with everything unloaded, Becca was finding a place in the fridge to put the juice boxes she'd bought for the kids, when he pinned her.

"Becca, I want to know what made you laugh earlier and caused that lovely blush." He was kissing the nape of her neck.

She shook her head and moved to shut the refrigerator door.

He let her but then trapped her against the wall holding her hands behind her back and started to attack her ears, driving her crazy.

His one free hand moved under her shirt and was playing with her breasts.

He whispered, "Tell me." As he continued building her desire.

"No, it was just a random and rather vulgar thought."

He let her go, looking frustrated and walked away… leaving her wanting.

AGAIN!

'Jackass!'

She didn't feel like dealing with 'Mr Fucking Moody' and went and made the bed with some of the now clean sheets. Once that chore was done, she decided a swim would cool her off and give her some space since he didn't seem to love the water as much as her.

He'd made that very apparent. More than once.

She went out the back storage room door and dove off the end of the dock and started swimming out five feet or so and turned to start her laps down past the bunkhouse. She stayed in the deeper water since it was easier to take fuller strokes and full kicks. Well, that and she was trying to antagonize Kane a bit.

*Rule breaking… AGAIN. Her specialty.*

On her third lap she looked up and he wasn't on the deck or the dock.

Huh?

Maybe he was over his phobia? That would make her life easier.

She was treading water when she heard the jet-ski, it was close, too close!

The stupid kid barely saw her in time to turn the front ski which still grazed her forehead. It could have been much worse.

Jet-skis are not allowed that close to shore.

'Fucking weekenders, never do obey the rules of the lake.'

Becca was beyond pissed and was now also bleeding.

She made her way to the beach and went up the other side of the cabin to the back door closest to the bathroom.

Head wounds always bleed a lot.

HUGE déjà vu moment.

She walked in and made it in the bathroom before Kane was off the couch.

She didn't know if he saw the blood or her expression. She locked the door.

She applied pressure and ignored Kane's knocking.

The bleeding stopped and she could tell no stitches were required but she'd have a nice bruise to accompany the cut.

She put a Band-Aid on it and went to call Jake.

When she opened the door, Kane took her head in his hands and looked at her wound.

"What the fuck happened Becca and why in the hell didn't you let me in to help?" Concerned and miffed.

She was just plain angry she pushed his hands away. "Maybe I didn't want to be fucked with again."

Walking past him she grabbed her phone and called her nephew.

"Hey Jake… yeah, he called… listen, some fucking kid just sideswiped my head with a jet-ski… about four feet past the buoy… I'm fine… no… NO… yes thank you." She put her phone down, the adrenaline was ebbing, and she started to shake.

Kane pulled her into his arms, and she felt warm and safe. She also apologized for being a bitch to him. He laughed.

"Jake coming?"

She nodded.

"I'm sorry too. I didn't realize you were even swimming. I heard you in the bedroom and then I found a Mariners game."

"Baseball over me. Sad." She was actually smiling.

"Never sweetheart. And if Jake wasn't on his way… I'd be proving that. How about we get you out of that wet swimsuit?"

He pulled her head up so he could give her a very nice kiss.

Kane gently touched her head and told her he wanted to kill the kid on the jet-ski.

She laughed since it really wasn't a capital offense but, if found, Jake would give him a nice ticket and stern warning.

She wrapped her arms back about him so he would continue holding her.

He did.

She loved how safe she felt within those two arms.

Her wet suit had dampened his shirt and they both went and put on dry clothes.

Jake and Justin arrived about twenty minutes later. He made her take the Band-Aid off so he could take a photo for the report he had to file. He looked mad.

"We've given half a dozen tickets for riding too close to shore in the last couple weeks. When will they learn?"

The JJ's didn't even have to go and look for this offender, his father was driving the noisy contraption with the kid on the back right up to the dock.

The kid looked scared to death. Of course, Kane was there, looking fierce and pissed plus Becca could tell by the father's expression that he wasn't expecting to find the sheriff's boat waiting.

'Tough shit.' She hated the weekenders, and it was only Thursday.

"Good afternoon. I'm Robert Baxter and this is my son, Alan. After he told me about the incident I wanted to come down and make sure that you were okay." He was speaking only to Becca it would appear.

Kane wrapped his arm around her waist pulling her close.

Before she had a chance to speak, Jake took over the conversation.

"Mr Baxter, I'm officer Sims. Did your son also mention that he was riding way too close to shore when he struck Mrs Jackson?" Cop voice.

'Oh, for fucks sake Jake, lighten up. The kid looked terrified.' She just might push him in the lake… gun and all.

She also would be talking to Kane regarding his possessive demeanor.

"Yes, officer that's why I brought him back to apologize and, of course, to cover any medical costs." He seemed sincere but Becca was getting a weird vibe from the dad. And the kid had a swollen lip.

Now, he could have had that earlier, she didn't get that good a look as he barreled down on her.

Jake nodded and Justin chimed in.

Well of course he did.

Justin was just over six feet and very trim. Muscular but not like Jake or Kane. He had very short dark hair with hazel eyes.

Very pleasant features but today his appearance gave him a true cop look.

*Yes, the uniform helps with that.*

"Alan I'm officer Grant, how old are you?" Cop voice.

Becca was now very happy that she had called them. Little hairs were standing up on her neck as she looked at Alan's father. She somehow knew deep down he was a creep, for this, she was a hundred per cent sure.

Having Kane's arm around her made her feel so much better and safer. He'd get a pass on his possessive behavior.

When the kid told them he was thirteen, both Jake and Justin gave a rather stern look to his father.

Kane tensed and Becca just felt bad for the kid. Her anger about the incident was gone. And truth be told she just wanted the Baxter's to leave.

Commence the full-on police scolding. "You have to be at least fourteen years of age to operate a jet-ski in these waters on your own and you must pass a safety course, which would have told you that you also have to ride at least fifty feet from the shoreline. Both these infractions are two-hundred-dollar tickets and Mrs Jackson does have every right to press charges." Jake was on a roll.

"Officers, this is totally my fault for letting him ride. I didn't read up on the rules and had no idea. We just wanted to have a fun family vacation, but I am more than happy to accept the penalties for these violations."

Mr Baxter seemed like a good dad on the surface, but just a gut feeling told her he was putting on a show. Call it woman's intuition but she wasn't thrilled that he knew where her cabin was. But happy that Jake called her Mrs Jackson, that way this 'asshat' would think,

Kane was her husband. Nice thought anyway but today, even better.

Time to get this damn thing settled so they'd leave.

Becca gave Jake a look and he nodded.

"Let's go with lesson learned. And Alan," the boy looked at Jake, "you can drive with your dad on the back but keep it away from shore. It's as much for your safety as it is for the residents around the lake. Okay?"

The boy nodded and smiled for the first time since he and his jerk of a father arrived.

Mr Baxter thanked them all and reached up and shook Jake and Justin's hands as well as Kane's and squeezed Becca's a bit too hard for her liking. No one else noticed.

He took off with a very relieved son on the back and Jake gave his aunt a nice hug.

"You're a good man, Jake. Thank you."

His grin so much like his dad's.

"You too Justin." Who was looking at her head.

"You're lucky Becca, that could have been so much worse. Nausea, listlessness or severe headache and you get to the hospital." Yep, cop tone.

Kane who had been very quiet, finally spoke.

"Thank you, gentlemen, but I've got this."

He shook both their hands and let Becca give hugs and led her back to the cabin as the JJs headed off looking for other rule breakers.

"Sweetheart, are you okay, really? You look off?" He was cradling her on the couch.

"I'm fine and I have you to take care of me." She pulled his lips to hers and thanked him for being much a loving and caring man.

She was so glad Kane was there. And hoped she'd never see Mr Baxter again. She seriously felt bad juju radiating off him. And her hand still hurt from his squeeze. 'Creep.'

It had been a very eventful day, so Kane heated up leftovers for dinner and they called it an early night.

# FRIDAY

Becca woke with Kane's arms around her, and she smiled, feeling safe and loved.

She hated that he had to work on that stupid yacht again but not everyone gets their summers off and really, this should be his busy season drumming up business to build new boats over the winter months.

She decided to give him another very nice wake-up call with her new found skill and moved out from under his arms and slipped down the sheets to her target.

She actually hated this act when she was married but quite enjoyed it with Kane.

He also must have enjoyed it since his moaning fueled her quest.

His arms pulled her up to waiting lips before her task was complete, but he had other ideas. "My turn."

Her moans fueled him as well and his tongue was taking no prisoners. She climaxed and, before that orgasm even finished, he was deep inside her. They came at the same time, and he laid on top of her catching his breath. She loved the feel of his weight on her and he was still inside her.

'What a great way to start any morning.' She was grinning.

Kane was giving her mouth a thorough exam with his tongue when they both heard the boat.

"Fuck. We'll have to finish this later my girl." And he pulled out leaving her a bit sad but still well sexed for the day.

'DAMN, I love that man.' She shook her head and went and grabbed her freshly laundered robe.

She started coffee before going out on the front deck to wave at the boys.

Kane surprised her by twirling her into his arms with a very passionate kiss.

"That had to be the quickest shower I've ever seen." Giving him another hug.

"Oh no, Beautiful, I didn't shower... I want to smell you on me all day." He winked.

He patted her ass and headed down to the dock as the boat came in to pick him up.

She was glad her blush couldn't be seen from that distance.

She waved as they took off towards their problem child.

Well caffeinated and showered, she sat in the living room drinking a shake.

It was the last one that Jake had bought her. She figured she might as well get back on track for at least one day while 'Mr Quirky' was busy.

She really did love Kane but needed him to lighten up about her food allotment.

She was wearing her new jeans and they were in fact a size ten and fitted perfectly. But she wanted to make sure they stayed that way.

She really was having a very good day.

Time to get ready for her nephew's visit; Mark like his dad, was a bit anal in regard to cleaning.

She dusted, vacuumed, swept, mopped and cleaned the bathroom thoroughly. She then went to make the bed. It needed clean sheets, but she didn't want to go back to town again to do laundry, so she opted for airing, drying and remade the bed with its current bedding.

*Oh DEAL! You know you've done it before.*

The sun was warming the day nicely, so Becca grabbed a water and headed down to sit on the dock for a bit of relaxation.

She was sad that this would be her second to last day before heading north.

'Maybe I should go to the high meadow before the invasion.' She couldn't help but think about the last time she was in the meadow. And blushed.

When she heard the boat, her heart leaped, Kane. NOPE!

Sheriff's boat.

She shook her head. 'WOW! I have it bad for him.'

"Hey Aunt Becs, just doing a welfare check." She smiled at her very thoughtful nephew.

"All good. Thank you, Jake."

She loved the little shit.

"By the way... you must have dropped this." And he tried to hand her the thirty dollars she'd put in his cooler.

She shook her head and refused the money.

*Mentioned earlier that stubbornness ran in the whole family.*

"Becca, I can afford a few drinks for my favorite aunt. Please take it back and where is Curt?" He looked ten years younger with that pleading face.

She took the money deciding to hide it in the Enclave for gas money and told him that the yacht was still having issues, so she was on her own for part of the day.

"Okay, well I'll see you tomorrow, have fun with Mark, Amy and the kids." He winked at her as Justin pulled away from the dock.

"WHAT!" Her eyes were large with her realization of what he said.

She heard him laugh out a 'love you' and they were gone.

"FUCK! FUCK! FUCK!" She was getting peeved.

She didn't want that crazy bitch to come.

This happened the previous year as well. Becca was told it would be just Mark and the kids and at the last minute his wife decided to come and keep an eye on everything.

The problem was, when she came along, she moped, didn't swim and bitched at Mark about everything. What the kids ate, how long they could stay in the water, how much they were in the sun and of course she made sure that Becca and Mark didn't have a chance to catch up at all.

Apparently, Amy wasn't a fan of water. She could swim, but just, and two years ago she wouldn't let Gail come with Mark and the other two because she didn't think anyone would keep an eye on the two-and-a-half-year-old.

During last year's visit the poor child barely got wet. Becca didn't get it either. Mark put his foot down with Ashley and Collin and they were now fish in the water, but he let Amy have complete control over baby Gail.

Not a parent, she had to let them do what they felt was right.

Still, she didn't like Amy. 'Not one fucking bit.'

And how her brother could stand her was beyond her comprehension.

Her phone ringing brought her out of her depressing and somewhat violent thoughts.

"Hello… you are a freak of nature, how the hell would you know I was thinking the 'f' word… did he now; well, I'll be dealing with my nephew at some point… FINE… yes I did eat breakfast… no… nope… I'm hanging up now… you know I find those arousing right… whatever… goodbye Mr Quirky."

She shook off Kane's call.

Now, how to get revenge on her meddling nephew for texting him that Amy was coming to the cabin.

She also didn't appreciate the inquisition regarding her breakfast or his threats of taking her over his knee. And he was laughing when she hung up.

'Jackass.'

Her phone rang again… 'What now?'

It was James.

'Well of course you'd be calling, Jake is going to pay for getting Kane and now his dad involved… jackass is just protecting his first born from my wrath no doubt.'

She was half tempted not to answer.

"Hi James and before you start with me, I'll be nice to the flakey witch so stop worrying."

"Well, he told me it was just he and the kids so, yes, it was a bit of a shock when Jake told me. Would have been nice if Mark grew a pair and told me himself."

"I would not have told him not to come… no he's not here, had to go fix another issue on that big-ass boat he built… yes it would… yep, you too. Bye."

'WOW! Little faith people.'

She had just under two hours until the brood would descend so a trip up to visit with the folks and her grandfather was more in order now than before.

The meadow was lovely with the morning sun shining through the trees.

She told her mom, dad and grandpa all about Kane and of course apologized for their indiscretion the other day.

Yep, she blushed again.

Feeling better after her mental chat, she headed down the road to stretch her legs.

She'd missed her walks and today would more than likely be the last one until next summer.

She'd made it maybe a mile and a half up the road when she heard her name being called.

'Odd.' And she didn't recognize the voice; she only knew it was male.

When she turned, she saw it was Mr Baxter coming towards her.

Shit, when he wasn't on a jet-ski he was a good three inches taller than Kane and carried a bit more weight and his arms were fucking huge. Ex-bodybuilder maybe. Blond hair with dark eyes… not someone you'd want to meet in an alley.

Not someone she wanted to ever see again, actually.

The hairs on the back of her neck were standing at full attention. She was getting a very bad feeling. VERY BAD!

"Good morning Mrs Jackson, I'm surprised you don't have your posse with you." His look wasn't at all friendly.

"Mr Baxter how are you on this lovely day?" She smiled trying to ignore the uneasy feeling she was getting from him. And the urge to run.

She was shocked when he suddenly grabbed her forearm; she tried to pull it away.

He squeezed harder causing her to wince from the pain.

His grip was unlike anything she'd ever felt. And she knew he could easily break her arm if provoked.

"I really didn't appreciate you calling the cops on my son for such a minor incident. Women always overreact. Perhaps next time you'll use your brain instead of your emotions."

He tightened his grip further causing another grimace from Becca.

"And just so you know, my family will tell the cops I never left the house today so if I were you, I'd keep your damn mouth shut for once!" He squeezed even harder making her cry out, he then twisted his grip and threw her arm to her side with enough force to make her stumble back and almost fall. He turned and walked away without a second glace.

She was stunned by his vicious and unprovoked attack. Her arm was throbbing, and her heart was beating a mile a minute. She was also feeling a bit nauseous.

Becca had no idea how much time passed before she calmed herself and looked at her arm.

It was beet red, showing his hand print and starting to swell. It also hurt like hell.

She now believed with certainty, that the fat lip the kid had was from his 'asshole' of a father.

Becca was still feeling scared but more pissed off at herself that she didn't mace the fucker.

'It just all happened so fast.'

With her senses back to their full capacity, all she wanted was to get somewhere safe. And with that thought, bolted for the cabin.

She ran as fast as she could but had to stop and puke, at that point she needed to walk for a bit and catch her breath.

She was never more relieved to see the lake house than that day.

Tears streamed down her face the minute she locked the back door. She locked all the doors and nursed a bottle of cold water trying to calm her nerves.

Her arm, which had swollen quite a bit more, was turning a nice black and blue.

It was currently wrapped an ice pack with the hope that would help with both the pain and the swelling.

She was shaking from the run and the shock of the malicious encounter. 'Come home Kane, please.'

She knew Jake would believe her side of the event, but the 'prick' was right... in the courts, it would be 'he said she said'.

She again made a wish for Kane to return.

All she wanted was his arms around her.

At that moment she realized just how important he was to her. He was her... everything!

The car on the hill brought her back to the here and now... it would seem that Dr Sims and his family had arrived, early.

Of course, they had.

'Great, from victim to hostess in sixty seconds. How in the hell do I cover this damn arm?'

"FUCK!"

She finished her water in one long drink and went and changed out of her tank top into a long-sleeved T-shirt. She also put the ice pack back in the freezer.

There was a small knock on the back door. 'SHIT.' She had forgotten to unlock it.

She opened the door and there stood a very sweet young girl with brown hair and the bluest eyes you've ever seen.

Her great niece, Ashley.

Becca got her first hug. "You've grown so much. I can't believe you're twelve already." Ashley smiled and moved to let a very precocious Collin, age nine, into the cabin to hug his great-aunt.

Gail was last but not least and she had her grandpa's smile and that instantly melted Becca's heart.

Mark looked a tab embarrassed and apologetic but gave his aunt a huge bear hug.

She whispered in his ear that it was fine and not to worry.

She could feel the tension leaving his body.

Amy got a cursory hug… that suited both women just fine.

"Aunt Becca, what happened to your head and why are you wearing a long-sleeved T-shirt in this heat. And where is this new man I've heard about?" Mark was too observant and a bit nosy for a dentist.

"Got a bump cleaning the loft... damn rafters and sunburn, you know me, and Curtis is working on a boat he built for a local resident up in Hope." She shrugged.

Plausible lies are always the best. And since she was the only one who actually called him 'Kane' she used his first name.

He shook his head and reminded her that they made sunscreen just for people who can't seem to stay out of the sun. And she needed to be more careful with her head.

She knew he was teasing her.

Unlike his brother, Mark took after his mother in looks.

Both boys were about the same height, but Mark had redder hair and his eyes were a smoky blue. He was also skinny as a rail, just like his mom.

Amy wasn't much over five feet and thin, almost waif-like. Except for her breasts... they were in fact quite large for her petite frame. She also had brown hair, but her eyes were a beautiful cobalt blue, and all three kids had the same color. It was her best feature.

"Aunt Becca, you look great by the way. I'm also sorry I won't meet the man who captured your heart." Mark was trying really hard to make up to her.

"Thank you, sweet boy. But you never know, he might make it back before you have to leave." She smiled.

"Now, is there anyone here who would like to go swimming?" She looked down at three very cute nodding faces.

Their mom insisted on sunscreen first and floaties for Gail.

Mark took his shorts off to reveal his suit was underneath and took the other two down to the dock with their towels. This was after they were thoroughly anointed with waterproof sunscreen.

As stated before, Ashley and Collin had grown up on the lake, just like Mark and Jake and, before them, Becca and James.

None of them were afraid of the water.

Just Kane and apparently Amy had a few issues.

Poor little Gail had less exposure to the water since Amy couldn't swim all that well and Mark for some odd reason didn't push the subject.

Stated earlier and still just as strange.

Just one more reason for Becca and Amy to be at odds.

Becca thought about getting on her suit and leaving the long-sleeved T-shirt on but was worried the bruise would show through, if wet. Disappointing since she would love to take a dip. The cool lake water would feel especially good on her hurt arm.

She opted for changing from jeans to shorts since it was very warm. She also remembered to unlock the very back door next to the bedroom.

Becs started to watch the kids from the upper deck in a little bit of shade.

Their carefree youth was a delight to observe as they played in the water with their dad.

Gail was also having a good time running on the beach and occasionally wading into the water and splashing her daddy.

Amy just sat on the dock watching her family but not joining them.

'Why the fuck did she even come? Oh well... she's the mom after all.'

Becca went white as a sheet when she heard a jet-ski. Her pulse rate only calmed when she saw it wasn't her earlier attacker.

She didn't see Collin come up the stairs but when he grabbed her arm she yelped and scared the shit out of the poor kid.

"Oh sweetie, I'm sorry. You just startled me. Are you okay?" She had on her best kid-friendly look.

His lip was quivering but he nodded.

She smiled and asked if he'd like something to drink.

He did.

She got up and fetched all the kids a juice and delivered them to the dock.

Collin had to wait until he was down the stairs so he could hold the railing. His aunt didn't want any mishaps on her watch.

Amy gave Becca another 'I don't like you' look.

She smiled and said it was one hundred per cent fruit juice. That seemed to appease the wretched woman.

Limited sugar… dentist for a dad.

Jake's arrival made her happy for several reasons. She knew he more than likely came back to give her a bit of moral support, but she had another agenda.

Mark's look was more perplexing. He seemed a bit hostile towards his brother.

"You two aren't fighting again?" Becca was looking right at Mark.

He blushed and shook his head.

"Good."

"Hey Mark, Amy… okay if I take a quick swim with my nieces and nephew?"

He is such a little brother.

He got a nod from Mark. Amy just ignored him.

*She really is a bitch.*

"Aunt Becs, my swim trucks?"

She pointed to the clothesline at the back of the cabin, and he was off like a shot.

She took that opportunity to go and talk to Justin for a few minutes.

"Permission to come aboard officer Grant?" She was smiling at him.

He nodded with a 'what are you up to' kind of look.

"Justin, can I talk to you about something without you going and blabbing it to Jake or any other member of my family?" She needed to gauge his response carefully.

"Yes, Becca, I can keep this between you and I." He sounded like her adopted nephew at that moment.

She sighed. 'Good'

Blocking her arm from anyone else on the dock, she carefully brought the sleeve up over her still very swollen and bruised forearm.

"Fuck Becca… this looks like a hand print. Who did this? Curt?" Wow, nephew to cop voice in a nanosecond.

"NO! Of course not." Trying to keep her voice down.

"So, you don't think I could just say I fell and got hurt."

Her look was hopeful.

"I don't see how. It looks like someone twisted your arm?"

She nodded.

"Becca, I should really file a report. This is assault. Please tell me what happened?" He was back sounding more like family.

*You could get whiplash talking to sheriff deputies.*

She gingerly pulled her sleeve back down and gave him a kiss on the cheek.

"I need you to let this go, please." And she climbed back on the dock.

Another jet-ski going by caused the same reaction as the first and this time witnessed by Justin and his look told her that he knew who hurt her.

Her eyes glistened and he nodded.

She mouthed a thank you and wiped her eyes.

She needed yet another distraction. Quick.

"Who's hungry? I thought we'd get some hotdogs going on the barbeque?"

In unison the kids all said, 'me'. Mark nodded and Amy just sat there, actually glaring at Mark.

*Seriously dude, no tits are worth that.*

Becca looked at Jake who was tossing his nephew a foot in the air before he landed back in the water asking him to do it again.

"No time but thanks. By the way what's up with the long-sleeved T-shirt?"

Before she could answer, Ashley told him her great-aunt had a sunburn and it hurt because Collin made her cry when he touched her arm.

'FUCK!'

"Really, well that is horrible." He gave his aunt a 'I know you're hiding something' look. She was wearing a tank top when they came by earlier in the day and knew for a fact, she'd not gotten a sunburn.

Observant little shit.

DAMN!

She shook her head and headed up to start the barbeque. This day started so very nicely and had gone to shit in a hand basket.

She was getting out the hotdogs when she saw the Bayliner through the kitchen window.

"KANE." And she instantly started to tear up.

'Stop this Becs. You need to feed the kids and not deviate from your plan.' She was still good at self-admonishing.

She went on deck and waved to him and the departing boat with Carl and Warren up on the flybridge.

He was wearing her smile. 'Damn I love that man. But I need to hold it together for a couple more hours.' Good pep talk.

Becca watched as he shook Justin's hand and engaged with little Gail who looked quite smitten with him. He also reached down and shook Mark's hand and Jake's before saying hello to Amy who, for the first time that day, actually had a brief smile.

He had that effect.

He waved to the other two kids in the water and took the stairs two at a time and folded Becca into his arms.

"Hi Beautiful." She was holding on tighter than normal, and it didn't go unnoticed.

"I'm glad you're back. I've missed you." Relaxing in his arms for the first time in what seemed like forever.

For the second time that day, Becca didn't see one of her nephews ascend the stairs. This one happened to be a cop.

"Curt, Aunt Becs lets go inside for a chat." Jake was sounding like his official self, in swim trucks.

Kane raised an eyebrow but followed the young man into the cabin holding Becca's hand as he went.

Before Jake even said a word, Justin barged in and told him to get dressed quick they had an urgent call out.

Jake ducked into the bathroom and dressed in record time, handing his aunt the wet swim trunks on his way out the door. He did give her a quick kiss on the cheek.

"Tomorrow we talk."

She nodded.

Becca asked Kane to start the barbeque while she went and hung up the swimwear her nephew bestowed upon her.

He gave her a peck on the cheek with 'I'm not it'.

She felt whole again now that he was there.

She would tell him the truth but after everyone was gone.

He deserved that.

She took him the hotdogs a few minutes later and he in turn gave her a very nice kiss away from children's eyes.

"I'm so glad you're back. How did it go on the boat?" She was still hugging him.

"Don't get me wrong sweetheart, I love hugging you, but I think it's a bit more, since that is the second time you've told me you're glad I'm back." He pulled her face so he could look at her.

"Can we please just get through this visit and then we'll talk." She pulled his lips back to hers.

"Okay. Well, the boat isn't fixed, but we think we narrowed down the issue so Carl will be on his computer the better part of the day and evening working on his software program. We have to go back tomorrow but it should only take an hour or so and I was hoping you might come with us." His look was so adoring.

She agreed instantly to his suggestion. There was no way in hell she was staying alone.

They were both surprised by the little voice asking for an ''otdog'. Grace was so very cute and a ginger like her daddy.

Becca adored the little girl. "They are almost ready honey; you want a bun."

She shook her head.

"Ketchup?" Received a vigorous nod.

Amy come out and took the little girl back inside.

Kane actually rolled his eyes and Becca told him she loved him.

He patted her ass as she headed back into the cabin with a few very lightly cooked hotdogs.

*You know, the 'why bother did you even cook them'... kind.*

She let Amy feed her kids since she knew what they liked. And she did promise to make an effort.

Becca was well aware that they limited the kids' sugar intake, 'dentist dad as mentioned earlier', but heard nothing about salt so she brought out the rest of chips from the prior weekend and all three kids dug in.

She also asked if anyone wanted chili on their dog and got a resounding 'no'. She knew Kane would, so she heated up the dish in the microwave.

After everyone had eaten and Becca did the few odd dishes since paper plates were used for the most part. Amy announced they had to be leaving and thanked Becca for her hospitality.

'BITCH!'

Becca noticed Mark's look of surprise at his wife's comment. More than likely, he thought they'd stay and do a bonfire so the kids could roast marshmallows for s'mores. That was where his aunt's thoughts were as well. After all, it was a cabin tradition. Ashley and Collin looked even more disappointed.

Mark excused himself and his wife and took her out back… Becca thought a trip to the woodshed would do that woman a world of good and Kane squeezed her hand bringing her out of that pleasant thought.

She shrugged.

When Mark returned, he was alone. "Aunt Becca, I'm sorry but it's best if we just go. Thank you for everything. It was great seeing you and nice to meet you as well Curtis." He gave his aunt a hug, shook Kane's hand, gathered up all the wet suits, the kids and headed up the hill.

Well, that had to be the most 'why bother coming to visit' she'd had all summer.

Still, she was glad it was just her and Kane in the cabin, alone.

James had left two beers in the fridge, and she went and got one, along with the ice pack.

She handed Kane the beer and put the ice pack on her arm over the shirt.

Both his eyebrows went up that time.

She was just about to explain when the sirens caught both of their attentions.

A second sheriff's boat went flying by along with the EMT boat. 'Wow, Justin wasn't kidding, there was something serious happening down the lake.'

"Wonder what that's all about? But to tell you the truth, I'm a lot more curious as to why you handed me a beer? And would you please show me the reason you require an ice pack on your arm?" He cocked just one eyebrow at Becca.

She gave him a very audible sigh. "Will you let me get through the entire event before you go ballistic?"

He opened the beer and agreed after taking a long drink.

'Here goes nothing.' She lifted her sleeve to reveal for only a second time what her arm looked like.

It was still swollen, and the handprint had faded quite a bit. Unfortunately, it had turned a very dark black and blue.

He took her arm very gently and examined it from every angle. He then put the ice pack back around it. But wouldn't let her hand leave his. "Spill it?"

"After your call and then my brother's, I was feeling a need for a little hike. So, I went up to the high meadow to chat with the folks and my grandpa. After that I went for a walk down the road and ran into Mr Baxter." She took a deep breath.

"He grabbed my arm and twisted it and threatened me. Told me not to call the cops. He scared the living shit out of me. And I forgot I had mace in my pocket which made me so mad at myself. Anyway, after he finally let go of my arm, I ran back here and locked the doors until Mark and the kids came." She couldn't read his expression.

He set the beer on the coffee table. "Thank you for telling me the truth. I take it no one else knows?" His color was changing to a vivid red.

She grabbed his hand with both of hers.

"Justin knows so please stay with me, I beg you, I need you close." She almost choked the words out in fear he'd leave and do something rash. Tears were streaming down her cheeks since her emotions were still a bit tattered.

His expression lightened.

"You know how much I want to find him and beat the living shit out of him! But Becca, I won't leave you. Not when you need me. I'll never leave you." He wrapped her back in his arms.

And, as promised, he held her for the rest of the night.

# SATURDAY

Last day at the cabin and she was feeling a twinge of sadness but also excitement to show her other town of Sitka, Alaska to Kane.

He was sleeping beside her, and she needed to thank him for holding her all night and staying with her.

She loved him so very much.

Her arm was looking a bit better, not as swollen but still very bruised.

Her thoughts were interrupted by Kane's phone. She was about to get up and get it, when he rolled out of bed, naked. Her favorite view.

He smiled since he knew she was watching his every move.

"Hello...? Yep... Damn it, Carl... fuck that... yes, pissed off is a good guess. I'm supposed to leave with Becca tomorrow. Fine. Don't push your luck, I said fine." He hung up and closed his eyes. His breathing was harsh, and Becca knew he was beyond angry.

Even with just the one-sided part of the conversation, she got what was happening. He needed to stay, and she needed to let him.

"You have to stay and take care of your business Kane. I really do understand. I'll miss you and I'll be waiting for you with bated breath the minute you can break free and come north." She was hoping to calm him.

He climbed back in bed and brought her lips to his. It was his turn to get lost in their love. There would be no talking for a half hour or more.

*Said it before and I'll say it again, moans don't count.*

"Becca, I just want to lay here in this bed making sweet love to you all day long. Would that be, okay?" He was massaging her shoulders.

She was smiling. "Too bad we don't have Joel here to cook for us."

He turned her over and looked at her. "Who's Joel?"

She honestly didn't know and told him she must have meant Warren and it came out with a totally fictional name.

Weird, but not.

"I like your cooking better." And he gave her a nice kiss.

"Why thank you Mr Kane, what would you like for breakfast? I can do pancakes and bacon or eggs and bacon. My apologies but we are out of sausage and ham."

"Pancakes please and I'd like for you to eat one with me." Not quite the stern look, but close.

She nodded since she knew she controlled the size. Sassy at its finest.

Kane got up and pulled on his pajama pants, she was again enjoying the view of that fine ass.

He threw her the white nightie that didn't really leave much to the imagination.

"I don't believe you've worn that one yet. It's all you'll need for the rest of the day. No robe Becca."

She blushed at the thought but at least it was a tad longer, almost to her knees.

She tested first, a little low but yesterday was unique to say the least.

Coffee time and she turned on the oven for the bacon and pulled out the grill.

Multitasking.

She took her turn in the bathroom once Kane was through.

He winked and nodded his approval of the new sheer nightgown.

Her grin got his attention.

"Just thinking how we are acting like such a normal couple, just feels good."

He pinned her to the wall, caressing her silky ass and taking full control of her lips and mouth.

"Oh no lover, we can do better than normal."

He let her go and went and got a cup of coffee.

'Fuck he's good.' And she worked at calming her breathing.

As they passed in the kitchen, he swatted her ass. "Thinking it." And chuckled.

She just shrugged since she was.

Bacon in the oven, pancake batter made… she got to work flipping flapjacks.

"Breakfast is ready. Would you like to eat in the living room?"

He came and sat at the table, and she served him his four, sort of uniformed, pancakes and four slices of bacon, pointing to the butter and syrup on the table.

He kissed her hand and thanked her.

When she sat down with her plate his eyebrow went up with disapproval.

Her pancakes were half dollar size but there were two with one egg and a piece of bacon.

It didn't take a genius to figure out that she'd waited until he poured syrup before she sat down.

His tone told her he knew exactly what she'd done.

"Eat every bite Becca." His look told her not to mess with him.

She was just finishing the dishes and Kane was behind her with his hands stroking the sides of her sheer nightgown.

His fingers could make her shiver so easily.

His tongue was playing with her earlobe. "Should I take you right here?" His whisper caused a fire throughout her whole body.

She reached behind and gently stroked his quite hard penis.

"Damn woman." And with that, he had her back on the bed where they enjoyed each other's bodies for the second time that morning.

'Death by orgasm. Worse ways to go.' She couldn't stop smiling.

By early afternoon Becca came to the realization that they had done nothing this day but stay in bed loving each other. It was bliss but she also knew she needed to pack at some point.

That brought reality to the forefront.

Kane was looking at her arm again and she knew he still wanted to kill the guy that hurt her.

"You never told me all of what Carl said on the phone this morning." Distraction technique number two, since they just had sex.

"Well, we have been a bit preoccupied. Thank you very much by the way." She loved that smile.

"The software glitch isn't quite as easy to fix as he'd hoped so he is currently rebuilding the program from scratch, and we will spend the better part of the week getting it installed and tested. The only good news is that the new owner is off the yacht for the next ten days."

"Don't move woman, I'm going to forage and find us a snack." He got up and headed to the kitchen, naked.

WOOF!

"Baby, what time is Jake coming?"

She responded, "Around six, I think."

He returned with the last piece of fried chicken, sliced cheese, two bottles of water and a cut-up apple.

"I didn't want to cook anything." He winked.

She smiled and took a piece of apple and a water.

After their picnic in bed, he floored her by suggesting a swim. Her exuberant response flabbergasted him as did her attack taking ownership of his lips.

Well, they eventually took a swim.

*Damn they both have some serious stamina.*

Kane was on the dock watching Becca swim.

She was thrilled he joined her, but the cool water got to be too much, and he opted to sunbathe while she finished saying goodbye to her lake.

Bittersweet to be sure.

He wrapped her in her towel when she climbed the ladder to the dock.

"Sweetheart don't be sad. You'll be back before you know it. And I'll be in Sitka in less than a week." She loved his hugs.

They both looked when they heard the approaching boat.

The sheriff's boat with the JJs. 'Odd'

Justin pulled alongside the dock and Jake jumped off pushing the boat back out and waving to his friend and partner.

Justin blew a kiss to Becca with a, "See you next year." He really was like her third nephew.

She yelled a 'love you J' as he was leaving.

"Hey Curt, Aunt Becs… you knew I was coming." Apparently, they both had a shocked look on their faces.

Only at the timing of his arrival, it was just after five.

"Sorry Jakey for some reason I thought you were coming later and not dressed like 'Officer Krupke'."

Kane laughed.

Jake just looked confused.

'Youth is totally wasted on the young.' And he really needed to watch *Westside Story*. She smiled.

The towel was hiding her arm but when she went to give her nephew a hug it slipped revealing her very bruised arm.

He held her arm for a minute.

"Justin told me after we arrested that cocksucker yesterday afternoon." He shook his head at his aunt.

"That was the callout we had to go on by the way. Took us over two hours to find his ass. Coward was hiding in the woods. We had to call in extra hands to search. He and one of the other weekenders got in some altercation and he beat the crap out of the guy... you might have seen the EMTs go by." Both Becca and Kane nodded.

"Becca, you should have told me yesterday what that jerk did." He gave her his stern cop stare.

She in turn gave him an, 'I'm about to throw your ass in the lake' look.

Kane shocked the crap out of both Jake and Becca when he pulled him into a hug and thanked him.

"You just saved my ass from going to jail, I wanted to kill the fucker."

"Stand in line Curt." With that he picked up his duffle bag and headed to the bunkhouse.

While Jake was taking a swim and Kane was watching a Mariners game, Becca got to work packing for her flight the next morning.

She decided to wear her new slacks and the one long-sleeved top he purchased for her just three days prior.

With her outfit for the plane set aside she finished packing all the other clothes Kane had generously bought for her. She spotted that lovely deep maroon negligee.

It felt silky and had a laced pattern down the whole back that was revealing in a very classy way.

She couldn't resist trying it on.

What a wonderful feeling garment against her skin. Becca continued wearing it while she finished packing the rest of her clothes.

All, except for the white nightie, it found its way into Kane's bag. Just a little reminder from her to hurry up and get his cute behind to Sitka.

She was going to miss him, even for such a brief amount of time.

She also didn't like the idea of living in Clara's house without her.

If Douglas was planning on living there as well, she'd move out immediately.

Kane's arms made her jump. "I am going to miss you my beautiful girl." He ran his hands up both sides of the silk nightgown letting her know that this was his favorite. And when he turned her around and saw the back, he actually growled.

"Stay right here and don't move." Yep, stern but sexy as hell.

She heard him open the front door and call to Jake. "Cabin is off limits for an hour."

She saw Jake nod as she shut the blinds in the bedroom.

He was back seconds later. "Now where was I?"

Lips, tongues, hands and 'DAMN!'

At least he was good enough to move her suitcase off the bed, so she didn't have to repack everything.

"Have you always had this kind of stamina?" She was curious and very tired.

"No. But taking a year off seemed to help since I worked out a lot." He was grinning.

She nodded in complete agreement.

Maybe she needed to join a gym.

Well, that was an unpleasant thought.

She pulled out the two T-bone steaks she'd picked up when she was in town on Thursday. Planning ahead was a wonderful thing. They got seasoned with salt and pepper only. Channeling her dad once again. 'Never muck up a good steak with sauce.'

She put two large russet potatoes in the oven to bake and got everything out to make a nice salad.

She even fried the last four slices of bacon so the guys could crumple them on top of their potatoes.

Jake and Kane were in the living room watching some other baseball game since the Mariners played earlier.

Well of course they were.

"Okay, who's barbequing this evening? And I have one beer left."

Jake volunteered for both.

He took the beer and steaks and headed out back.

Becca got the table set and even made a couple of biscuits to complete the meal.

Jake was back twenty-six minutes later with steaks cooked to a nice medium rare. 'Good boy.'

Never overcook a good steak.

"Damn woman, dinner looks amazing." Kane then proceeded to cut a nice piece of his steak and put it on her plate with her salad.

She smiled and they all dug in.

Both men ate everything including the potato skin. She enjoyed watching them eat.

Kane smiled when she finished her meal as well.

*Of course, she did, she'd had quite the workout, most of the day in fact.*

After she was done cleaning the kitchen and organizing the fridge so Jake and Justin could see what was in there, she wiped down all the counters and got the coffee ready for the morning.

Once she wiped off the table, Jake reappeared with Monopoly and a shit eating grin.

It was his favorite growing up and she remembered how ruthless he was as a slumlord.

"Go ask Kane." She couldn't help but smile.

She loved the little shit.

Kane came in and took a seat at the table asking to be the top hat. Becca couldn't help but laugh.

Another fan of the game.

It was just after midnight when Becca kicked Jake out of the cabin. She'd been beaten by both men and owed Kane several thousand in past due rent. She usually lost but not quite as badly as she had that evening.

She set the alarm on her phone for five a.m., which would give her a chance to get a shower and drink at least two cups of coffee before the trek to the Spokane International Airport.

Kane wanted to come, and Jake said he'd drop him at City Marina to meet up with Carl and Warren once they were back.

She had everything packed for the most part and her carry-on had a jacket, iPod, headphones, her book and a small jewelry box. She'd throw in her testing kit and meds in the morning.

Still a bit sad to leave this amazing place.

She reflected on some of her childhood memories and all the new ones she had from this wonderful summer as she locked up and turned out the lights.

When she entered the bedroom, Kane was standing with his arms open.

She walked right into his embrace and felt loved beyond belief.

He made love to her that night, but it was so much more, and they both felt their passion take on a whole new dimension. Even their climax was so much more tangible.

She drifted to sleep in the arms of the man she would love forever.

# SUNDAY

She woke to Kane giving her kisses. "Becca, I am going to miss you so very much." He proceeded to move his kisses down to her breasts and her whole body surged at his touch.

She wrapped her legs around him as he gave himself to her.

They were in sync with every move, every kiss and shared the powerful release.

She was catching her breath when the alarm went off.

'How in the hell did he time that so perfectly?'

She reached over and brought his lips to hers. "I love you Mr Kane."

"And I you Ms Sims. I booked my flight for a week from today, flight sixty-three… arriving in Sitka around one thirty p.m. I will count the minutes." He then gave her a very intimate kiss and told her to go get in the shower.

She did as she was told. Starting the coffee on the way.

*Priorities people.*

Tested, dressed and packed she sat down for a much-needed caffeine infusion.

She also changed the sheets.

The ones she removed seriously needed to be washed or burned, take your pick.

Kane was sitting beside her holding her hand.

"When did you book that flight? Did you not sleep?" He shook his head.

"I watched you sleep. I wanted to memorize every curve, every freckle and every hair on your body. A week will be an eternity." He kissed each knuckle on her hand.

She was melting at his touch.

Jake came through the door like a freight train. "Morning!" And proceeded into the bathroom.

Tender moment displaced with laughter.

She barely got in a second cup before she was ushered out the door by Jake. Kane was more resistant.

She had just enough time to say goodbye to her lake, the cabin, and the memories of her mom and dad and, of course, her grandfather.

"Okay, I'm not playing chauffer so you two can sit in the back and suck face all the way to Spokane so let's have Kane drive with you in the front seat and I'll catch another twenty winks in the backseat." Jake was smiling at them both.

'He knows *On Golden Pond* and not *Westside Story*.' She smirked at him.

"I am quite fond of sucking your aunt's face but since we are a threesome in the car, I'll be happy to drive." Kane had a huge grin on his face.

"No, you won't! You got no sleep last night so I'm driving, and you both can nap." She actually put her foot down.

Both men gave in, smart decision!

The drive was quiet, and she thought both Kane and Jake were asleep as she turned onto the highway leading them to Coeur d'Alene. From there she'd get on Highway ninety to Spokane and her final destination.

Kane squeezed her hand.

"I thought you were sleeping?" He shook his head.

"Tell me what was so funny the other day outside the laundromat?"

His thumb was making circles on her hand… she loved his touch.

"Kane, it was a random and crude thought." She knew he wasn't going to let it go.

Jake was snoring softly in the backseat so that made her feel less apprehensive.

She sighed. "Fine… When you said you felt emasculated, I sort of thought about a dog with his tail between his legs… and then putting your anatomy into that analogy… made me think of the limerick, 'There once was a man from Nantucket'." She was blushing.

He started laughing and woke up poor Jake.

"Sorry Jakey, go back to sleep." And to her surprise he did.

Kane's grin had turned a bit wicked. "We never discussed that possibility, maybe something to consider once I'm in Alaska."

"That isn't happening. Sorry but OUCH!"

The thought was actually terrifying.

He laughed again but not loud enough to disturb her nephew.

"Okay... a topic for another day." His grin was still evil.

She knew she shouldn't have told him... this was not going away.

By the time she made the freeway, both men were out cold. She was lost in her own thoughts for the last forty-two miles.

By the time she pulled into the airport, both Kane and Jake were wide awake and arguing with her about coming into the airport.

She made the suggestion that they just drop her off and got a very loud 'no' from them both.

Goodbyes were hard enough. Her way was more like pulling a Band-Aid off: quick.

Being outvoted two to one, she parked and handed the keys to Jake.

*She forgot one year and almost boarded with them. Being a cop came in handy that day since he got to go through security without a ticket.*

She walked arm in arm with Jake and her other hand firmly holding Kane's.

Once checked in with boarding pass and her luggage in the capable hands of the airlines she said her goodbyes.

Huge hug from her nephew with a kiss to the cheek and his signature, "Love you Aunt Becs."

Jake walked away giving her and Kane some privacy.

He pulled her into his arms and whispered, "I love you Rebecca Lynne Sims with every fiber of my being. I hate letting you go." He brought his lips to hers.

"I love you Curtis James Kane and I'll be waiting for you in Sitka one week from today. And I'm not saying goodbye. I'll see you soon." And gave him another kiss and turned to head through security.

She fought tears the whole way to her gate.

# EPILOGUE

Becca was waiting right outside the arrival exit, which in fact was a bit of an oxymoron, but still.

She had butterflies waiting for Kane's plane to land at the Sitka Airport.

It had been just one week since they kissed goodbye in Spokane, and she had to board Alaska Airlines alone.

She missed him... his smile, his arms and those lips. She was so looking forward to kissing those lips.

They'd only spoken once since she'd returned. He'd been busy getting that glitch on the yacht fixed so he wouldn't be delayed any longer than necessary.

*It worked out nicely since she was doing lesson plans and getting ready to start her first class of the semester.*

*Plus, Douglas was planning on living at his mom's house, so Becca had to scramble and find a new place, quick. She got lucky and found a one-bedroom apartment over another professor's garage. Little more rent but a lot more privacy. And with Kane coming, that was a huge plus.*

They announced the arrival of flight sixty-three from Seattle and her heart took a huge leap.

She was ever so glad that Sitka had a short runway and was a very small airport.

This flight would continue on to Juneau so she figured only a dozen or so people would disembark. One being the man she loved.

*Ever notice that when you are eager about something, time seems to go in slow motion?*

Frustrating was not even close to what she was feeling.

Finally, the plane was pulling near the terminal. 'YES!'

She was looking for her man when she got distracted by a former student saying hello and asking if she was coming or going.

That made her laugh for a whole different reason but graciously told him she was picking up her boyfriend.

Not even close to the truth but 'love of her existence' sounded a bit ostentatious.

When she turned her attention back to the exit, people were now making their way through.

She felt flush and her heart rate picked up... anticipation and adrenaline.

When the last passenger walked by her and into the arms of the woman standing just behind, she just stared at the exit.

'Where was he?'

She waited.

They called for the boarding process and soon flight sixty-three was taxiing away from the gate on its journey to the capital city.

And she was still just staring at the exit.

'WHERE was he?'

Her heart began to hurt, and she picked up her phone in the hope there was a message from him.

'Why didn't he make the flight? OH NO, did something happen?'

Her heart starting racing again but now it was in panic mode.

She quickly dialed his number and got 'this number is not in service'.

'Shit, I dialed the wrong number.' And she carefully dialed Kane's number a second time... again she heard some faceless harpy tell her that 'the number was not in service'.

Her heart stopped or at least that's what it felt like.

She wanted to sob but couldn't.

She was having trouble breathing.

"Where are you Kane?" She almost choked it out.

Her world was crumbling around her, and she felt like her heart was breaking.

Her whole body was shaking.

She thought someone called her name but there was no one around her.

She felt herself shake even more and again heard her name, somewhere in the fog of her mind.

"Becca! Becca! Wake up! Come on baby, I'm right here Becca." Kane was shaking her gently.

Her eyes fluttered opened, and she was in bed and Kane was looking down at her with worried eyes.

"KANE!" And she pulled him on top of her hugging him as hard as she could.

He pulled back and gave her a very nice kiss.

"Bad dream baby? You were calling for me and you sounded so scared. I've been trying to wake you. I blame that damn cold medicine I gave you." His look was concern and slightly amused.

She nodded.

And pulled him back to her lips.

"Becca, your heart is already beating quite fast from your nightmare. Let's get it calmed down before we increase it again." He was looking at her again with concern and that slight bit of amusement.

She took a couple of cleansing breaths. Never taking her eyes off the love of her life.

He was there and they were in bed.

The bed felt bigger, different, she could hear water lapping and she relaxed a little.

She felt safe in the arms of her man.

"What were you dreaming about?" He gave her another tender kiss.

"I dreamt that I was at the cabin, and you were there and my brother James and my nephew Jake. But then you and I got separated for some reason and I was waiting for you, and you never showed and then I couldn't reach you. I thought I lost you forever. And the pain I felt was beyond any I've ever felt."

Tears filled her eyes as she told him.

He wiped them away. "Just a bad dream brought on by the medicine which you are never taking again. Besides that, I'm not going anywhere without you so that scenario is never going to happen babe, ever."

His kiss was much more forceful as he amplified their passion.

She welcomed his tongue and her heart beat increased but this time with desire.

She was lying in bed with him, it was only a bad dream that was now drifting away into her deep subconscious, and they were making love.

It all seemed a little different, but everything still seemed right with the world.

Back in his arms and feeling beyond loved in every way possible, she had her eyes closed and was listening to his breathing. Her favorite sound. She was caressing his very firm stomach. Almost too firm, but not.

She shook off the wayward thought.

"I love you with all my heart Kane." And kissed his chest.

His arm tightened around her.

"And I you baby. Now and forever." Cane picked up her left hand and kissed her ring.

She smiled and looked at the lovely Alaskan lovebird ring…

'WHAT the FUCK!'